Mad Scientist Journal: Spring 2017

Edited by Dawn Vogel and
Jeremy Zimmerman

Cover Art and Layout by Luke Spooner

CONTENTS

ACKNOWLEDGMENTS

Many thanks to Patreon backers Simone Cooper, Andrew Cherry, John Nienart, Torrey Podmajersky, and Michele Ray!

LETTER FROM THE GUEST EDITOR
by Malevelous Vile M.D., Ph.D., D.D.S.

Hello worms,

I've been asked to welcome you to this magazine. Presumably with some pleasant words about madness, science, whatever.

Instead, I would like to talk to you about teeth.

In my weapons program, I have been cultivating a way to use sonic beams to shatter all of the teeth in a person's mouth from up to five hundred yards away.

It is a very delicate bit of calibration. If you do it wrong, you could shatter the skull, and where's the fun in that? You can't see the look on their face if you do that. In fact, there isn't really a face.

Some people have said to me, "Mally, why would you do such a thing? That's a lot of work just to destroy teeth."

And the answer is simple: it is fun. Without a certain *joie de vivre*, why bother putting on your hazmat suit every morning? Death is so easy to bring. Any idiot can build a bigger gun. But suffering? That's an art that gives meaning to an otherwise pointless existence as we drift ever onwards into entropy.

- MV

Dr. Vile studied medicine at the Harvard School of Law, impressing faculty and staff with his ruthless ability to coerce a medical degree out of the most unlikely of places. He is currently wanted in 27 countries for crimes against humanity and overdue parking tickets.

1

ESSAYS

STHENO
An essay by Stheno the Gorgon,
as provided by Marnie Azzarelli

———

"Brave soul, walking by herself in *this* neighborhood at night,"
the passenger in a gray mini-van commented to her driving friend
as I crossed the intersection in front of them. *They are more afraid of
me than I am of them.* I smiled, holding my hands within the confines
of the dark, hooded sweatshirt I always wore, shivering a little to
show how cold I was. It only mattered if they perceived I was cold,
even if my breath didn't come out from under my hood in a puff of
body heat.

I tried to walk too quickly for anyone to truly notice. But I
needed someone to *see*. That lady driving home with her friend
noticed. She was concerned, and a little disappointed that I would
think walking around the South Side at night was a sound idea. Her
worry and inevitable twinge of envy were unfounded on me. I have
seen so many women like her, all the same, all scared of the endless
dark sky that created shadows where the streetlights ended, hiding
what needed to be hid from view. It is their enemy, and like all evil,
there was an irresistible draw that tried to hide away.

I do not blame them. I was just the same once, but time has a
habit of forgetting stories like mine. I walked farther down cracked
sidewalks where weeds found new life in every split. The
convenience store on Mulberry was open, its fluorescent lights
cutting out a rectangular shape so cleanly against the night that the
inside of the store looked like a living picture framed in black. The
man behind the counter was surrounded by a Plexiglas cage, while
more people in sweatshirts and thick coats picked up snacks and
cigarettes. I crossed the street before I got too close to the glare,

and made my way down the block.

Those women were right to rapidly drive away. The South Side functioned only as a part of town to pass quickly through, especially if you didn't belong on its streets. Most of the small shops that dotted the road I traveled down were either abandoned or fronts for many illicit practices, and "shady" didn't truly capture the characters that walked around at night. It is dangerous for even the ones used to the place, but the disappearance of many girls had been its most recent issue. They were always out walking at night, when it was too cold and too dark for any act of bravery. They would be followed as they traversed the block and stolen at the corner, or chased until they were found somewhere else.

I bet that's why that woman made her comment. The ones who live away from this side of the city don't understand. While death is the ruler of this tiny hamlet, the ebbs and flow of gender, class, and race change its target. As time passes, predators find a new prey. The next day could prove to be the end of terror for young girls who liked to look at the night sky or buy a snack at the convenience store on their own, and I can only guess at who would be next.

I made it to the corner where the street lamp flickered and faded and found myself smiling through tight lips. The corner hotel was the most beautiful place in the area. Well, beautiful to me. Down in town, the buildings were much larger and grander, and as they grew, the South Side shrank with all the money funneling into the center of town.

But the building I loved wasn't so fancy or expensive. Shaped like a tall brick box a couple of stories high, its only adornments were the windows on each floor as square as the building itself, and a large wooden door in the middle. A sign hung from a post above it, a large lit square with the visage of a big smiling cat covering it completely. The Laughing Lion Hotel, covered in ages of dirt and ivy, was the only place I cared about in the world. I had never truly gone through its front door or visited the bar off to its side that always seemed busy, and I never dared to slip into its private rooms to witness the many private things that went on in them, but I loved it just the same. Making my way to the corner, I walked by the lovely building, whose two sidewalk trees always covered it up from most of the neighborhood. And as I strode by, I dared to take a hand out of my pocket and raked my long nails across its outer

6

wall, where the moss and grime released the scent of its age. It reminded of a home I missed.

I turned the corner and went around to the back of the hotel, where a derelict building across the darkened alley hid a drug den and housed the homeless where a smashed streetlamp gave them a little privacy. I started down the alleyway behind my beloved when laughter forced me to shake my shoulders and jump back to where the light from the corner still hit.

There is one thing in this world that will always stay the same: a man who wishes to do a woman harm will always present himself in the most ridiculous way possible. I saw his smile first as he tore himself away from the shadows. It was large and white. In a different setting, his smile would charm, cajole, engage, seduce. But at night, it had a different effect. It couldn't cover his intense smell that radiated off of him like hot pavement. He didn't seem to have a home indoors with running water, or so he wanted me to think.

That stench no more belonged to him than it did me. His body, tall and lithe, moved closer to mine, and I could truly smell him underneath his clothes. He was clean and sharp. No scent of sweat or years of awful hygiene. When the light fully revealed his face, his eyes glowed deep amber, and I could see dirt smeared on his face. It was all too deliberate—his skin shined beneath the filth, and the cap that supposedly hid his glossy hair was just as deliberate. *They* were truly all the same.

He barely spoke above a whisper, the sound starting somewhere deep in his body only to bounce lightly off of those perfect teeth. "What a brave soul you are."

I ran.

Past the hotel, past the convenience store, past the intersection. I glided, I flew. I could feel him two steps behind me. The scent from the clothes he stole filled my nose. I made it down one more street, only to stop in front of a working street light right in front of an alleyway. It was another perfect spot for him. I beat the breath out of my lungs, let my eyes widen, shook my shoulders, and twisted my head while spinning around. I was the face of abject terror. My sisters would be proud.

He stopped at the edge of the light, and I pretended not to notice. He chuckled again, throwing his voice so it bounced all around me. I panicked a little more and turned away from him. I couldn't hold it back any longer. My shoulders shrugged and my chest heaved. Water came forth from my eyes, and I made a mewling sound that would break any man's heart. Inside, I was laughing, and laughing, and laughing. I was so brave.

I knelt, letting my laughter take me to deeper states of despair, the sounds of my choking sobs covering up the sounds of his footsteps from behind. I was so brave to let him come closer and closer, hearing that large smile curl the edges of his lips as he exposed his gums to release the fangs that lived there. Sharp and fresh. Before he could even think of lunging, I turned and fell on him, throwing him into the alley only to straddle his flailing form.

I slammed his steel-strong shoulder against the pavement, snapping it as he howled. I covered his glowing eyes and pushed his head to the ground.

He tried to snap his teeth at me out of anger and confusion.

"You should have known better." My voice was barely a rasp, age taking its toll. "You must be young."

He growled and spit, trying desperately to move. He wasn't used to it. For centuries, he must have dominated and purged the world of beautiful young women. He didn't know about me. Never could. Only the ones so old they turned to dust knew of my true existence. My true power.

I lifted my hand away and let him see. I didn't look directly at him, but I could feel his reaction as I showed him my true face.

The face I wear is not real. I peeled it off piece by piece. The full pink lips, a well-shaped nose, round supple cheeks, large doe eyes, all fake. I shook it all off so he could see me.

He stopped flailing to stare, unblinking.

I wondered how long it had been for him to fear. To look the unknown in the face, and know that it was real. I pulled my hood down to let my red hair tumble out in waves that undulated on their own accord, hissing in tandem with the rasp from my throat.

"Mein Gott." He let go of his façade. The nobleman he truly was came to surface as he threw his arm over his eyes, more dramatic than anyone of this time. His histrionics showed his age. He was hardly 300 if that.

I pulled his arm away with a strength that sobered him as I spoke, throwing my voice into a hollow echo that I knew he could feel through his body. "Do not be brave, mein lieb. I would never harm you." Although my voice no longer held its strength, my music was still there. It is a music that reminded him of childhood, with rolling hills, and rich dark soil, of kinfolk long gone.

He swore behind his teeth.

He had a music of his own that calmed and charmed women to do his bidding. My music was much more than his. He lowered his arm and gazed into my eyes. He screamed when he took in the full horror of my being. Even to him, a monster, I should not exist. I let him cry out loud. He chose the right neighborhood to hunt in, as a scream in the night would never be answered. As his face turned gray and hardened with the force of my eyes, I placed my mouth on his and took what was mine.

It is a common misconception that these creatures are dead. No, no, a human cannot hear it, or see it, but the immortal's heart still tremors, its lungs carry the tiniest bit of air, and the blood that largely did not belong to it runs through its sluggish system. They may be strong, and quick, and hellishly evil, but they are just a pest, less than a human, more like a bug.

And they do have souls.

So far down that not even they know of its existence, there is a small, albeit corrupted soul. And as his lips grew harder, and rougher, less of steel, more of cement, I took it from him, and kept it with all the others like him.

When I was done, I slid off his solid body and gathered my face from the ground as he began to crumble into the concrete. Another common misconception. They do not stay stone for long. That would be wildly impractical and highly conspicuous. Sometimes they don't even turn to stone at all. They only become one with their setting. Some have turned to mud, others to wood, and one even turned to ash, but they all go.

They must because they don't belong anymore, not when they cause so much destruction. When he was gone entirely, I placed my face into my sweatshirt pocket, and stuffed my moving, angry hair underneath my hood.

I walked back to the Laughing Lion, and into the alley behind it. I went down its full length, averting my eyes from the truly homeless as they slept outside. I found the entrance to the crawl space of my beloved and slipped inside. My home was not very large, but the rocks I called walls and the dirt I called a floor was perfect for me. It reminded me of a home so far from the South Side.

When Medusa was beheaded, I was lost. She had been my rock,

so to speak, and while I knew her mortality would get the best of her one day, I still grieved. I left Euryale to drown in her own despair and ran. I travelled the world and watched the humans tear each other apart, but I also saw their kindness, beauty, and truth. They were hidden among the chaos, secret shadows that I needed to dig for, to find in dark spaces.

The owner of my beloved hotel treated me well and let me stay like his father did, and his father's father, and his father's father's father, and so on before even the Down Town was created. He never really talked to me, and never looked at me, but he let me stay. Why wouldn't he? I did try so hard to keep the neighborhood safe.

Stheno was born in the caverns of Mount Olympus and is the eldest sister to Eurayle and Medusa. She was transformed into an immortal Gorgon when Medusa was assaulted by the sea God Poseidon in the Temple of Athena. After Medusa was beheaded by Perseus, Stheno fled from Greece to travel the world. At some unknown time, she finally settled in the south side of a small Pennsylvania city where she resides in a rundown hotel and protects it from any threat that crosses her path.

.

Marnie Azzarelli's short work has appeared in *Clever Girl* magazine and Marywood University's literary publication, *The Bayleaf*. She has co-authored a book entitled *Labor Unrest in Scranton*, which was published in 2016, and writes plays for local theater productions. She holds a B.A. in English from Marywood University, writes scary stories that only scare herself, and reviews TV shows that keep getting cancelled. Azzarelli currently lives with two cats, two parents, and one dog in Scranton, Pennsylvania.

A GIFT OF LIFE AND DEATH
An essay by Mira Delmer,
as provided by Caroline von Schmalensee

Last night, everything changed. I'd got to the bit where I tell Roland about how I met his father when, out of the deep blue, he said, "But Kraken's a myth. He's not real."

He's six—it could have happened at any time. I knew one day he'd start to question my stories. There's no room for Kraken on land; humans don't believe in such creatures.

My face went cold and tingly, my eyes filled with tears. "He was mythic, alright," I said, voice too deep in my throat, "but not how you think. No one has caught him on camera, sweetling, that doesn't mean he doesn't exist. Mm. Mythic. That's the word."

I went on with the story, but Roland wasn't really listening, and I sank into a sea of memories, quietly mourning the boy he had been and the telling of our tale. I had lost my son to a world I have no place in. "He doesn't exist"—what a thing to say about your father. The implication is clear: I, as I was when we met, didn't exist either. I'm a liar.

When Roland was younger, he stuck to the script that proved we belonged not to the world outside, but to each other.

"So how did you meet my father?" he would ask.

No, that's not where the tale starts. It goes like this:

"Once upon a time," I'd begin, "there was a mermaid who lived in the deep, deep sea. That was me."

Roland had the most beautiful smile. Sitting on the side of his bed, I'd stroke his head, marvelling at the heat of him against my much cooler hands. We'd worked out a routine, a way for both of us to tell the tale. The next line was his.

"Were you a princess?"

"No, sweetheart, nothing so fancy. I was just a normal, drop-dead-gorgeous mermaid, one among, oh, hundreds."

"Did you have long hair?"

"I had very long hair, much longer than now, of a glossier gold."

I miss the hair. If you had asked me, before, I wouldn't have guessed that I would. Except the hair I have now is not the same. Back then, my hair was longer, smoother, more gold than straw in colour. Still, some nights, if I've had a bad day, I'll hide Roland and me in a tent of hair. If I close my eyes, I can imagine that it still smells of salt and fish oil. Sitting in a hair tent is like looking out at the world from inside a thicket of pale seaweed. It makes everything look friendlier, less threatening. We're here, my boy and I, safe, despite the air all around us.

"What did you do all day?" Roland would ask next.

"I did what mermaids do: I combed my hair, gambolled in the breaking waves, and sang to passing sailors. My sisters and I would swim with the dolphins—if they weren't too frisky, dolphins are naughty animals. Or we'd chase sharks or cruise with whales."

Here I'd pause, put my hands to my chest, and add "I liked singing to sailors the best" with a coy smile.

"Was that how you met my father?" was Roland's next question.

"In a way, my wee sprat. But he wasn't human."

I'd turn solemn, eyes serious, mouth unsmiling.

"We live like humans now, and you'll grow up to be one, but that's not what I wanted when I was young. My lover was Kraken, a majestic creature with a solid, muscular body, and arms that could wrap around and sink a sailing boat. His skin shifted in all the colours of the rainbow, and he had eyes the size of my head."

Roland's little blue eyes would be round with amazement.

"Tell me about Kraken!" is what he'd say, the day before yesterday, while he still believed.

"Your wish is my command. Kraken's squid-like—" I can't help but smile when talking about Kraken; the very thought of him warms the cockles of my heart. "—only much more handsome, larger, more intelligent, and oh so strong! He is the most amazing creature I have ever encountered. So smooth, so full of life and will."

"I was charming a sailor, swimming around his boat, singing to him, showing a little bit of shoulder, a little bit of a smile." I'd give

Roland a taste of the smile, famous in my father's court. There, it sparkled. I still have a great smile, but it's lost something in the translation to human flesh. It can turn the heads of men and women alike, but I rarely use it for that purpose. What can they give me, other than food? We have nothing in common. I tried making friends with some of the mothers at Roland's nursery, thinking the burning love of our offspring would help tie a lasting bond. It didn't. Their chatter bores me; they find me weird.

"The sailor was leaning over the water, holding on to the rigging of his little ship and gazing at me, eyes deep with longing. I knew it was just a question of time before he jumped. I dove under the boat and called to him, making him scamper across the deck to see more of me."

It doesn't take much to recall that day: the fresh scent of salt on the air, the smell of plastic and varnish clouding around the boat, the softness of the breeze tickling my skin. It was a golden day.

"I was raising my upper body up out of the water, standing on my tail, draping my golden hair around me, when something moved in the water. The sailor gasped and fell back. Two tentacles flanked me, moving with me, like dancers copying my movements, one on either side. They were pearly white, with just a hint of pink, a perfect match to my skin."

It had been a beautiful sight. I was deeply flattered by the gesture. Who wouldn't be?

"I'd seen him around, as a shadow in the deep, far away in the murk, a muscular shape flitting through the water. We danced for a few seconds. Then I dove down to see him. His body was under the boat, and when I came near, he pulled his arms close and flushed a beautiful deep rose. Then, in a second, he was away, changing his skin to all the colours of water. I followed. He led me deeper than I'd ever been, tantalising me with his shape and colour. Then he stopped. I swam close to him, stroked his forehead, lay my body along his. He stroked me with his tentacles, first gently, then more passionately. Our courtship was short but intense."

I'd stop there, reel myself back from the memory and take a deep, abridging breath.

"We married. That very night."

Kids don't need all the details.

Roland and I would smile at each other and applaud the union. It's my favourite part of the tale, a moment of pure happiness.

"In the sea, marriage isn't like it is here. We didn't set up house, cling limpet-like to each other. We lived at different depths and ate different foods, had our own lives. We simply loved each other."

Truth is, I still love Kraken. The sweetness has turned to bitterness, but it's love all the same.

"We'd meet every evening in the mid-depths to talk, hunt, and dance. Some nights I'd sing, and he'd illustrate my songs with his tentacles. It was magical. We enjoyed each other's company—each other—more than I can say. Our joy was complete. We were happy all day, looking forward to meeting, and blissful all evening, together in the swell of love."

It was up to Roland to break the mood. "But it couldn't last."

With a sorrowful shake of my head, I'd agree. "No, it couldn't. Kraken is his own lord; he does whatever he wants. I was a mermaid. My life was lived at the whim of my father. And he wanted to use me to form an alliance with a nearby lord. One of my sisters told him I had married, dashing his political plans."

"She was a snake!" Roland would hiss, scrunching up his face and sticking his tongue out like the cutest little water snake. He always made me laugh.

"Indeed, she was a viper, a serpent, a traitor most foul."

I had other names for her, names I didn't share. She'd petitioned our father for marriage to her sweetheart seven times, each time receiving a rejection. Not that I cared: I didn't like her much either. My sister didn't like me in the first place, and when she found out about me and Kraken, she exploded. Our mutual antipathy sent her straight to dad, tittle-tattling.

"Oh, he was furious! Beside himself!" I'd screw up my face into a ferocious mask, showing sharp teeth, making claws of my hands. "In a fit of rage, Father sent his men to kill Kraken. My husband and I were chasing orca, diving from warm top waters to chilly depths, herding a pod towards their doom. Suddenly we were surrounded by fierce mermen, poking us with tridents and churning the water to show their displeasure. Kraken grabbed one after one, squeezing and shaking, before dropping them, unconscious or turning to jelly and glass."

"Glass like this?" Roland would ask and hold up his favourite toy.

His toy is special to both of us. It's the size of my fist, its surface is smooth with shallow ridges running top to bottom. It's transparent and cool to the touch. Underneath the surface, four chambers show, each opening out into a tube on the surface. It's a heart. I've told Roland it's the heart of a sea-serpent, a ferocious foe.

"Exactly like that."

I haven't touched it for years. If Roland held it too close to me, I'd nudge his hand away, and he'd tuck under the duvet.

"Many sea creatures melt into jelly and glass when they die, that's why so few sea-serpents and merfolk wash up on human shores. We become sand: mermaid hearts and bones ground to powder by time and tide."

It's a fact. Oh yes, it's made up of ground down rocks and bits of shell too. If you look closely, through a microscope, you'll see grains of surpassing clarity. They are tiny pieces of my kind.

"That fight was the last time but one that I saw my husband. My father's men couldn't hurt Kraken. But they could hurt me. They caught me and took me back to my father's court in the city of pearls."

At this point, my eyes would glisten with tears. Even after all this time, it hurts me to think of what my father did to me.

"The king didn't bother with a hearing; he summarily banished me to the land. A vile potion was forced down my throat, and the scales fell from my tail, the bones splitting and changing until I had these lumpy things."

To Roland, and anyone else, these legs of mine look as good as any human legs: strong, long, and softly rounded. To me, they are a hideous disfigurement. I never wear trousers: why would I emphasise the unsightly split? I like my skirts long enough to hide my feet.

"The worst was when my gills closed. I only just made it to the surface, gasping like the fish I had been, unable to swim properly, every breath burning my lungs, strange noises coming from my throat. Luckily, I was picked up by a passing sailboat. It was the sailor I flirted with the day I met your father. He didn't recognise me. Everything about me had changed: my hair had fallen out, my skin had gone sallow, and I had legs."

"Poor Mummy," Roland would say and stroke my hair. My misery was making him sad too; it was time to sing a cheerier tune.

"It wasn't all bad—" I'd smile and kiss him. "—because I took you with me out of the sea. I arrived on land with a boy in my belly, and that boy was you. The potion I took also changed you. And here we are."

What happened to me after I reached the surface wasn't something I included in the tale. There's a point when honesty turns to cruelty. I have a version ready for when Roland is fully grown, if he asks, and if he wants to listen.

The sailor who found me took me to land, where I got medical treatment. It didn't take me long to pick up the local language—mermaids are good at mimicry. They didn't know what to do with me: I didn't fit the description of any missing person, and I didn't know who I was. There was no point telling them where I came from, because they couldn't help me back there. I was in exile. The confusion I showed was real. After a period on a psyche ward, I was released into what they call "the care of the community." I was on my own, eight months pregnant. I was scared of giving birth—I'd seen whales calf. What an inelegant baby delivery system! That's not how my species delivered our young.

I had expected to deliver an egg—one perfect, heart-sized egg, round as an octopus' eye with two sinuous tendrils, one at either end, that I'd use to fasten it to a rock or seaweed, somewhere warm and safe. I'd visit the egg every day, croon to it and caress it, until, one day, my baby broke the membrane and swam out into my arms.

Instead, I sat on a sofa in a social housing flat, caressing and crooning to my belly. Every day I got a little bigger, and my fear grew a little more urgent. I tried to be calm: I was stuck on land, forever banished from the sea. I had to make the best of the situation, and the best was the safe delivery of my child.

I gave birth in the bathroom, on the floor, with much heaving and groaning, screaming and wailing. After a muscle-ripping push, Roland slid out of me like a pup out of a seal cow, in one smooth motion. I gathered him to me, crying at his human ugliness, and fell asleep suckling him.

The next day, after cleaning up myself and the bathroom, I swaddled Roland in a T-shirt and dressed. I walked down to the harbour, to the very end of the pier, where the water was at its deepest. There I sat down, holding Roland in my arms and calling for his father. All day I called, pitching my voice at a register that would travel far in water.

Some of the fishermen tried to get me to go home. I looked like a mad woman, clutching my baby, keening at the horizon. I think they worried I'd hurt myself or Roland. Deep inside, some of them recognised me for what I was. They were men of the sea, after all. I answered their questions politely, accepted gifts of tea and fish, but refused to move. Eventually they left me alone.

The sun went down and the moon rose. I stayed where I was, calling.

He came.

Dark tentacles rose from the water. Outlined in moon silver, they undulated like dancing mermaids in the greeting he had especially for me. It made me cry to see him so close.

My body had changed, but my tastes had not adjusted to its new form. They never will. Kraken remains the most beautiful creature in my world and, that night, I missed him with an intensity that wiped away the aches and pains of my labour. I wanted to dive into the water, into Kraken's arms. I looked into his big eyes, just visible where they reflected the moonlight from under the green-black water. I'd seen his eyes in moonlight before but never from this side of the surface. I cried harder, anointing our child's brow with nacreous tears.

I unwrapped Roland and held him out over the water so his father could see him. The moonlight made his skin shine herring-belly white.

All my pain, my sadness, I kept from Roland. How he met his father, and how he got the heart, I was happy to tell.

"Kraken rose closer to the surface, raising a tentative tentacle towards you. He'd brought you a gift. I had to snuggle you into the crook of my arm to receive it in my other hand."

Roland would bring out the toy again, and we'd look at it. Intricate and strong, it glittered coolly in the light of Roland's blue reading lamp, the light seeming to pool in its chambers.

I remember lifting the heart so clearly, water drops like roe clinging to its surface. It beat—once, twice. I gasped and looked at Kraken. The movement was a message. Merfolk are magic. Even in my changed form, the heart recognised a direct blood relation, parent or child. There was only one heart it could be.

"Thank you," I sang to my husband, squeezing the glass heart in triumph. "Thank you!"

I haven't touched the heart with my bare skin since that day. I know who it is; Roland doesn't need to. He has to grow up to altogether softer feelings than the rage I brought with me out of the sea. I gave the heart to him, watched him cuddle and gnaw it, like babies do, then play with it as he grew.

In a way, the heart is the end of the story. It is the lesson I want Roland to take with him when goes to his own life. And yet, because of where we live now, it is a lesson I can't allow myself to teach him. Instead, the tale ends with singing.

"We stayed there, looking into each other's eyes, me singing, Kraken dancing, until the first ray of the sun touched the bay with gold. It was a sad farewell but it had to be. He loved you so much," I'd assure Roland, stroking his head to feel his life under my palms. "I know he wished he could be with us."

We'd hug, and I'd sing him to sleep.

"There is no greater gift of love," goes the song, "than a gift of life and death."

I'd repeat those words, varying the melody, until Roland's eyes closed and his breathing deepened. Every night for six years I'd leave him sleeping, his cheek resting on his grandfather's still heart, and close the door behind me.

I won't tell the tale again, not tonight, not tomorrow. That chapter of our lives is closed. But maybe I'll still sing.

Six years ago, Mira Delmer was banished from the Oyster Court by her father for marrying Kraken. Since her exile, she's been building a home for herself and her son, Roland, on land. Mira has difficulty fitting into human society but does her best to ensure Roland will grow up a happy, normal boy. She's currently exploring employment opportunities as a professional story teller.

Caroline von Schmalensee lives in Edinburgh, Scotland. A technical writer by day, she writes fiction in her free time. Caroline writes urban fantasy and makes forays into fairytale and horror. Her short stories can be found in *New Writing Scotland*, *The Seven Wonders of Scotland*, *The Scotsman*, *FREAKCircus*, and online. She's working on her first novel.

Caroline writes about writing at carolinevonschmalensee.com.

MRS. HOBGOBBLE'S GRADE 5 TROLL HOMEWORK: TOOTH FAIRY EXPERIMENTS
An essay by Johnny Trollson, as provided by Sarina Dorie

Lab Partners: Johnny Trollson, Trog Pixiestomper, and Glurp Swampbottom, Grade 5

Biology Class: Tooth Fairy Experiments

Purpose:

To determine if a tooth fairy survives after her wings are torn off.

Research:

Because tooth fairies store magic in their wings, tearing them off will render them helpless and turn them mortal. Mortals are susceptible to death. According to the textbook, wing removal is painful and kills some species of immortals. Others survive for brief amounts of time, lasting no longer than a hundred years. That is, if a troll doesn't intervene first.

Hypothesis:

The tooth fairy will die a slow and painful death if her wings are removed. We will take joy in her suffering. At least, my lab partners will.

Experiment:

- Capture three tooth fairies. Make sure to take away their wands and disarm their charms and glamour spells so they will not trick the researcher with any shenanigans.
- Place each of the fairies in separate cages.
- Leave both wings intact on the first fairy. Record how long it takes her to die.
- Remove one wing from the second one. Record how long it takes her to die.
- Remove the full set of wings from the last one. Record how long it takes her to die.

Observations and Analysis:

We learned that tooth fairies are difficult to catch. Actually, that's what my lab partners learned. I told them this at the beginning. Back before I was forced to come home to the troll caverns, my fairy godmother showed me tricks for avoiding trolls, ogres, and feral unicorns. Unfortunately, I wasn't careful enough. My biological parents caught me and brought me home.

The textbook didn't say how to catch a fairy. There weren't any in the science wing in coolers like with the frog prince dissections. That was a relief, at least. My lab partner, Glurp, suggested prying false teeth out of a pair of dentures and putting them under her pillow. I knew it wasn't going to work. That trick has been tried too many times by human children.

I'm supposed to make an educated guess why it's so hard to catch a fairy. I think it's because they are smart.

In order to catch a tooth fairy, we had to stalk a human child with a loose tooth, wait until the tooth fell out, and then wait for a tooth fairy to arrive. Not only did we have to do this once, but we had to do it three times to catch three separate fairies. The worst part was when they tried to pull off the wings. Not because that icks me out—ahem, I am completely over my time spent living among kind, peaceful fairies and am now a well-adjusted troll who wishes nothing more to crunch human bones between my teeth and stomp on innocent pixies.

Each time something went wrong. The first fairy slugged Trog in the face with a bag of quarters and gave him a set of braces to remember her by. I don't know how the fairy got her wand back. It must have been set too close to her cage. The second one whipped out a wand she'd been hiding and shouted, "I'm not leaving until those teeth sparkle." She used magic to brush Glurp's teeth until her gums bled. When they tried to pull the wings off the last one, the fairy shouted, "I'm here to collect some teeth, you elfing hogboons!" She punched Trog in his already aching jaw and knocked two teeth loose. I suggested Glurp needed some wisdom, and that may have been why the tooth fairy gave my lab partner a set of erupting wisdom teeth.

Oops, my bad.

Conclusion:

Trog and Glurp don't want to ever see another tooth fairy for the rest of their lives. But that may also have had to do with the avalanche of teeth that came crashing down on top of them.

The tooth fairies told me if I was good, they'd be back for me. I can only hope. I will put Trog's teeth under my pillow tonight.

Johnny Trollson is a fifth-grade student at Snorgwog's School for Trolls. After being kidnapped from his family by a wicked "fairy godmother," he has finally been returned to his rightful family, where he spends his leisure time playing Kick the Head off the Leprechaun and eating humans. At least, that's what his parents tell the neighbors.

Sarina Dorie has sold over 100 short stories to markets like *Daily Science Fiction*, *Magazine of Fantasy and Science Fiction*, *Orson Scott Card's IGMS*, *Cosmos*, and *Sword and Lase*. Her stories and published novels have won humor and Romance Writer of America awards. Her steampunk romance series, *The Memory Thief*, and her collections, *Fairies, Robots and Unicorns—Oh My!* and *Ghosts, Werewolves and Zombies—Oh My!* are available on Amazon.

By day, Sarina is a public school art teacher, artist, belly dance performer and instructor, copy editor, fashion designer, event organizer, and probably a few other things. By night, she writes. As you might imagine, this leaves little time for sleep.

You can find info about her short stories and novels on her website: www.sarinadorie.com.

BIRTHING FIRE

An essay by Dr. Henrik Ahlstrom,
as provided by Dantzel Cherry

DR27-6 wobbles one last time, and a crack laces across the marble shell, etched by a small egg tooth. White and red fluids spill out. The tooth saws back and forth a few times, then stops.

I dim the lights and wait.

Another few moments and an azure head pops out—a male, then. His slanted copper eyes shift around the room.

He's calm, which means he hasn't recognized me as a threat yet. I know the cameras and monitors are at work, so I wait patiently. One step onto the heated rocks, then four more in quick succession for the rest of his body to be free.

Something threatens him—the basking bulb, presumably—and he releases FP144. Moving at such high pressure from the oral glands, the FP144 compound bursts into flames and I measure seven inches. I suppose that makes DR27-6 the fiercest, strongest specimen in this round of the project, but this is not enough to get my hopes up. He will likely end up like the rest. His fierce eyes, though ... they burn with life.

The blue on his head spreads downward and shares space freely with marigold until intermixing with crimson on the sailfin. His wings are beautiful, and functional—at least in theory. They're useless in the first few hours of life. Once we engineered functional wings in stage 2, we added the gene expression inhibitor to turn off the God-given poison production in the oral glands, and added the FP144 gland specific inducer in stage 3, which doesn't agree with the neurons required for flight. I convinced Tom to speak with Monsieur Benefactor about being content with flying, non-fire-

23

breathing dragons, but Monsieur was quite insistent.

Officially we name them with sterile, passionless identifications such as DR27-6, so that's what I record for Tom and the herpetologists. But alone in the basement like this, wild eyes glaring at me, he is more. DR27-6 is Fafnir, the strongest dragon of them all.

I should stop reading so much.

Eventually Fafnir looks for his first meal, stalking over to the plates under the warm lights and investigating his choices: superworms, fruit, pellets, fresh fish. He hovers over the wriggling superworms, smelling, considering. He snatches one from the plate, then another, and another.

He eats until he is full, then prowls about his enclosure. He stops by the same basking bulb that startled him earlier and stares at it in apparent contentment this time. I wait, hoping he will act differently than the others at this point. The scientist in me knows I should be fully invested in this experiment's success, but it's a heavy toll to watch the fire burning out of a creature that's lived for so long in our imaginations, yet only takes a few hours to die.

After a seven-year PhD and two post docs, I work for Monsieur Benefactor, who has no intention of letting Tom or me publish our work these last nine years. Sometimes I argue with the pragmatic Tom about our agreement, outraged that when—if—this is completed to Monsieur's satisfaction I'll have a great deal of money from his private accounts, but I won't be able to account for all these wasted years on my résumé. I rage about Monsieur keeping these sorry creatures secret for himself and his select friends. Other times, I look at the specimens I am tinkering with and am relieved no one knows what I've done.

I forget about Monsieur when Fafnir's wings, warm and dry at last, stretch open, preparing for flight. A breakthrough!

This time, I think, the FPI44 gland inducer and the neurons threading from his brain to his wings finally agree; they can coexist in the same body. Fafnir is only moments away from fulfilling his destiny—my destiny. I swell with pride. Perhaps Monsieur and I are more similar than I'd like to admit.

The wings pull downward, a flapping motion from a baby. He lifts off the ground for one glorious moment.

And then Fafnir jerks his head side to side, no longer the strange but normal bobs of a healthy lizard, but that of a dragon in seizure. He convulses and shoots out more FP44. The flames scorch the superworms and they writhe about, just like Fafnir.

Again and again Fafnir vomits fire, simply because his neurons will it so. His feet pull him around the enclosure, frantic, and he slips into his water pan. Flames still shoot out, sometimes stunted by the water when the angle is right, and sometimes not. I struggle to record this part, but cameras and monitors don't catch everything the human eye intuits, so I continue. I wish Tom hadn't missed today's hatchings—he detaches himself from this so much better than I.

The FP44 built up in Fafnir's body is nearly depleted, and so is his energy. His head droops into the water pan. I fear he will drown himself. I can't be a scientist now—maybe I could for DR27-6, but not for Fafnir. My hand shoots out and pulls him away from the water, though I consider whether drowning wouldn't be quicker and kinder than the tortured breakdown of brain and body.

Even as I expect that awful stillness to enter his body any moment, Fafnir, trembling, lifts his head and sniffs the air. He stiffens at whatever he smells and bites down on my thumb. I flinch but fight the instinct to fling the creature away.

Though those small teeth draw only a few drops of blood, Fafnir laps the deep red liquid until my thumb is clean. Again he bites and licks my wound. I dread a third time, but he seems satisfied. No longer shaking, my dragon stretches his marigold wings luxuriously and flaps them against the air, flying in a clumsy circle before landing back in the safety of my outstretched palms.

Two incubators away, Fafnir's brother DR27-8 wobbles into life.

After earning a PhD in Cell and Molecular Biology from Stanford University, Dr. Henrik Ahlstrom completed a post-doc at University of Virginia Center for BioTechnology and another at Scripps Research Institute as the primary investigator for the groundbreaking paper, Directed Induction of Foreign Tissue Growth in any Eukaryotic Host. After a short stint as Chief Scientific Officer for Bilon Therapeutics, he has since been involved in an undisclosed research project for a private laboratory in Belgium.

Dantzel Cherry teaches Pilates and raises her daughter by day. By night and naptime, she writes. Her baking hours follow no rhyme or reason. Her short stories have appeared in *Fireside*, *InterGalactic Medicine Show*, *Galaxy's Edge*, and other magazines and anthologies.

"Birthing Fire" previously appeared as the 2nd place winner in the Story Star Publishing Short Story Contest in 2012.

WAITING

An essay by Riley, as provided by Eddie Newton

Waiting. Always something difficult for me. I am more of an instant gratification kind of personality. But I learned a long time ago that there are some things worth waiting for.

All sorts of people waited. A septuagenarian with a deviated septum sniffed as she sat in a seedy settee. A garrulous gentleman going on and on about the impending elections offered her a crimson kerchief. Three little sisters that may have been separated by only a year sat in a neat row, blonde, blonder, and blondest in order of age, still and silent as they waited for a name to be called. The mother was pale as paste, hair sculpted from gray clay, attire a collage of contrasting colors like some demented diorama: chartreuse shirt, cerulean scarf, scarlet satchel, indigo earrings.

There were looks. Always looks. From the first time that I stepped out the door on Winston's arm, we garnered looks. Sidelong glances, muttered opinions, insinuated insults, even overt invectives. We weathered withering vilification because at the end of every day, love wins.

Until it doesn't.

A nurse came into the waiting room and called a name. A thin middle-aged man with a massive mustache and silver sideburns and only thin strands on his skull answered, stood. As he passed us, he made a face of disgust. We were a progressive couple, and the balding man was traditional from his khaki trousers to his brown bowtie. Winston shrugged off the sanctimonious sneer, but as always, it made me fidget and wane.

"We're next, Riley," Winston observed, taking my hand.

Colors collided. His skin was light and bright against my dark

27

complexion, like the interior of a peach holding the brown pit at its center. Winston was beautiful: every freckle one I knew by heart, each imperfection evidence of an ever-changing appearance, new scars simply accentuation of experience.

"Are you sure about this?" I asked.

Winston nodded without hesitation. "They say it is the only way we can be together. I would do anything to make that happen, Riley."

"I know," I said.

The world was not ready for couples like Winston and me. Shunned, shamed, accused of immorality, our love was a precarious predicament, something natural that had become a trial. We were judged injuriously, accused unjustly, and suffered unsolicited scorn. Just because we did not fit the mold. Ever something different, the world always searched out new subjects for subjugation. Once upon a time, the public would have declared deliberated disdain due to differences in race. As America moved on, mixed marriages became commonplace and society looked for someone else to eschew.

Antipathy was a seed that blew in the wind, finding purchase in new fertile grounds, growing into something strong and shady until society chopped it off once again. Then the seeds moved on, to virgin grounds, growing again, fresh shadows cast by reaching branches and myriad limbs.

"Your hair is pretty," said a little girl no higher than my knee.

"Thank you," I said.

It was brilliant blue, a punchy primary that recalled bright paints from an age before brushes. This toddler was surely acquainted with the tone. She probably thought my coif was art that belonged pinned to a refrigerator. Against my cocoa complexion, it appeared as blueberry topping on molten chocolate.

"What's your name?" I asked.

"Tennyson," she said. "Like the number ten, but spelled with letters."

I nodded. Most of the kids her age might have been 10yson. I have seen kids named 1der and N8 and S-6 and 2d. Progress can sometimes look like nonsense.

"Tennyson," her mother snapped, as she looked up from her electronic device. "Get over here."

"I am just talking to this nice man," Tennyson whined.

"We don't talk to strangers," the mother scolded. "No offense."

No offense. The great American lie. Two words uttered only when someone intentionally offends. The mother meant *strangers* as "strange" rather than "unacquainted". I was stranger in appearance than anyone else in the waiting room. My skin was dark as night yet bright with an incandescent glow and my hair an unnatural azure, like a bright clear midday sky over darkest night. With eyes uncharacteristically un-brown, instead a soft gray like winter ice, I looked more alien than indigenous. There was strange, like the teen with tattoos of tarantulas crawling across her exposed torso, or the elderly woman who shaved off her eyebrows and redrew them in crooked rainbows that made her appear perpetually surprised, or the young man who inexplicably waited wearing only a towel. That was all strange; I was stranger.

Tennyson toddled away without another word. Her mother gave her a second device, and the parent and child sat side by side sucked into a digital trance. The real world could be as weird as it wanted as long as they could retreat into their virtual refuge.

"Things are going to change," Winston promised.

"I know," I agreed. I just did not know when.

Indeed, the seed of antipathy blew on winds of change, but direction was indecisive, and sometimes a preternatural calm descended as the world held its breath. Bluster or dead calm, the momentum of any movement could be arrested for eons or gust forth in a tornado of transformation. Were we in a moment stuck in the muck or at the precipice of whirlwind revolution?

Waiting.

We were in the waiting room.

The nurse came back. He scanned the room. Winston started to stand, but the nurse's eyes skipped over us. Instead, he called the name of a meek myopic matron that looked like she had been around long enough to have suffered some serious animosity herself. She had skin darker than mine, hair as silver as a dime, and wrinkles that revealed experience measured in multitudinous decades. She might have marched for civil rights in her youth. Maybe she campaigned for marriage equality. She had certainly withstood the winds of change, witness to cycles of discrimination. As she passed Winston and me, she looked down on us, a disgusted puff of stale stagnation wafting by like a backdraft. Sometimes the winds of change blew in the wrong direction.

"I guess I was wrong," Winston said. "Surely, we are next. We have been waiting longer than anyone else."

Indeed, the list of people that had been called before us was long. A couple that had been discussing religion behind us had argued the entire time they waited, the wife a devout Catholic and the husband an Orthodox Jew. They bantered about their conflicting pious plans for Sunday before they were called, as they were called, after they were called. They were summoned long ago, both of them favoring Winton and me with a glare that suggested we were doomed to damnation. Next the nurse called was an impossibly white woman who surely shunned the sun and her two children, obviously biracial, blessed with more of their father's brown tone than their mother's alabaster affliction. She steered the children away from us as she walked by. After the white woman was another couple, one woman Hispanic and hotheaded and the other Asian and preternaturally calm. They had insulted each other in raspy whispers the entire time they waited, something about infidelity and indiscrete infections and endangered matrimony. One of them looked ready to spit on us as they passed, and the other just put her nose in the air.

"Maybe it is a sign?" I asked.

"You don't believe in 'signs,' Riley," Winston said.

"I believe what is right in front of my face," I replied. "None of these people are on our side."

"People are only ever on their own side, Riley."

A gargantuan mother of a newborn babe sat across from us, nursing and eavesdropping simultaneously. The infant was so small compared to his parent that he looked like one of those parasitic lampreys that latched onto the underside of a large shark. The mother scowled at us, making a face as if we were stink. Her face puckered into an unsightly orifice, like a supercilious sphincter. If she wanted to say something, she wisely kept her asinine assessment to herself.

The nurse returned. "Winston Price?"

We stood and approached the nurse. He looked like we had both showed up for the prize after only one lotto number was called. One of us had to be mistaken.

"Which of you is Winston?"

Winston stepped forward. "I am."

"Follow me," the nurse said curtly.

We both followed. The nurse looked at me like I had stepped in dog droppings and proceeded to tramp the residoo-doo down the clinic's white tile hallway. "He's with me," Winston assured, although the nurse did not appear placated. I still followed Winston deeper into the labyrinth of the clinic.

The nurse stopped by a door that looked like every other door, and opened it, standing aside to let us enter. His job as escort was over. Winston entered without comment, but I was less apt to hold my tongue.

The nurse frowned at me like he tried to figure out if I was merely abhorrent or the devil himself.

"You have a problem?" I asked.

"It's unnatural," said the nurse, student of medicine and everything homeopathic.

How far had the human race evolved? Once upon a time, people shunned relationships that were interracial, interfaith, intercultural. Then hatred of differences transformed into a loathing of sameness. The public denounced same-sex marriages. Then different and same were both acceptable, and the world agreed that polygamy was the new sin. *Was there no line sacred?* the remaining zealots cried.

So they found new ways to perpetrate hate.

"Nature goes beyond trees and birds and rivers and intolerant individuals," I said.

The nurse shook his head and walked away. I entered the room where Winston waited. It was not the antiseptic office I expected. Usually these places were small closets with a bed papered over for prodding and probing, a small desk to deliver bad news, and charts of innards adorning the wall like morbid modern art. But this was an actual office. As big as our living room back home, with a desk more appropriate an executive than an examiner, the room featured fine furniture, plush carpet, windows opening on a stunning view of the river, and actual artwork signed by renowned artists.

"What a jerk," I fumed, sitting next to Winston in a seat nicer than anything we owned.

"An ignoramus," Winston opined, "is best ignored."

"This nation has managed four female Presidents, two of them openly gay. The current Pope is a biracial trans woman. America does not even discuss the color of skin anymore. You can marry a man or a woman or one of each and no one bats an eye," I ranted.

"But we are so ostracized that you might think we were bringing back cancer."

"There has always been intolerance," Winston sighed, as if he was resigned to reality.

I wanted to reshape our situation until it conformed to our dreams.

Wasn't that why we were here?

The doctor entered. She was of indistinct appearance: hair washed-out brown, eyes an undetermined hue, not too heavy or too thin, age somewhere between thirty and sixty, average nose, face, posture, everything. She offered a hand as unremarkable as the rest of her.

"Dr. Merriweather," she introduced. "I am pleased to finally meet you, Riley."

Dr. Merriweather took a seat behind her opulent desk. The desktop was immaculately organized, pristine piles of paperwork, pens placed parallel in the corner, files laying flush and flat. Flattering Winston, she said, "You look good, Mr. Price." Finally, we were done waiting.

Winston was almost thirty, fit for his age and of a complexion that made him look younger than his years. Women especially seemed attracted to his appearance. There had been many a female admirer that barked up that wrong tree. For a moment, I thought that Dr. Merriweather was just another bitch. But the interest in her eyes was not in his physical form. The doctor was interested in something else.

"I feel good about this," Winston said.

"Are you sure about this?" the doctor asked. "This choice is not an easy one."

"We want to get married," Winston said.

"There is time," Dr. Merriweather cautioned. "The tide will change. It always has before. Surely, it will again."

"We are on the wrong end of a revolution," Winston declared. "The headwinds will take decades to change. Unless we can prove that we have just as much right to love who we love as anyone else."

"The world is not going to accept legal marriage between a human being and a Hard Light Construct anytime soon," I chimed in. "Unless there is incontrovertible evidence against prohibition."

"The laws of the land are explicit," the doctor advised. "A Hard

Light Construct is essentially without form, and as such is soulless. The rights and privileges of the United States are precipitated upon the assumption of personhood, the essence of spirit that dogmatists call a soul."

"The genesis of the argument is that HaLiCons are soulless," Winston said.

"No one can prove otherwise," I pointed out.

"No one has proved otherwise," the doctor corrected. "Yet."

I looked at Winston. He looked at me. He knew what he signed up for. It sounded like science fiction. But wasn't science fiction just a truth that hadn't happened yet? Winston insisted we come here to see if it was possible. I did not want to see him disappointed. This was the moment of truth.

"So you can prove otherwise?" I asked.

"That is why we are here," Dr. Merriweather explained.

When Exco Shakespeare invented a construct made of vibrating beams of light, it was revolutionary. Solid light, able to do physical work. Machines made of lasers. At first, the Hard Light Constructs were used in place of heavy machinery, or in toxic environments unfit for flesh, or as infantry in the last of the global conflicts. Technology evolves, so HaLiCons became personal assistants and assisted care for the elderly and nannies for America's toddlers. Then HaLiCons became a part of society. Then something more.

Winston and I were not the only ones who wanted to marry. There were thousands of couples across the nation comprising one human and one HaLiCon. We were a minority, but the originations of innovation ever began with just a brave few.

The government disliked the idea. The Powers That Be argued that marriage could not be sanctioned if one participant was a soulless machine. A Senator last session had famously argued that "man is not meant to marry a rainbow." But a HaLiCon was more than just an amorphous play of light. The Construct was just a shell that contained personality, emotions, attitude, aspirations.

"All our preparations are complete," the doctor said. "This is it. The waiting is over."

"Are you sure this is going to work?" I asked.

The doctor appeared entirely genuine. "There are no guarantees when you explore the unknown, Riley. It is not without risks. We have spent the last two years mapping every aspect of Winston's personality and functionality. But we are going to do something that has never been done. I have to upload his entire being into a new body. This is an attempt to disprove the government's argument. How else can we prove the point besides to demonstrate that there is no difference between a human and a HaLiCon? If Winston survives the process unchanged, it will illustrate that a construct is just a construct, whether created from flesh and blood or pure light."

But what if the Winston that came out of the hospital was not the same man who walked in. I took his hand. He squeezed it reassuringly.

He looked into my eyes and promised, "Everything will be all right."

Dr. Merriweather discussed final details with Winston while I wondered about the future. If we could prove the government wrong, then everything changed. Would Americans marry money? Would there be matrimony between a man and his meatballs? Could someone have a wife that was a waterfall or a husband that was a rubber band? Did this erase the line?

But that line always moved anyway. It had been blurred so many times that different people saw it in different places, like a ghost that haunts. I just wanted to love the man that I love. Consideration of incidental casualties was someone else's problem. They should not have stood between me and my happily ever after.

"I think we're ready," Dr. Merriweather announced, standing and heading for the door.

Winston stood up, looked at me with that look, and that was our last chance. Wait or go? Change our mind and head home and let someone else pioneer this new and scary world? Or step through the doorway that Dr. Merriweather offered, finding either the future we wanted or a fate we deserved? If the doctor succeeded, we dared to insult God. I feared the ramifications of impertinence.

I nodded. I was done waiting.

Dr. Merriweather led us along an empty corridor to a room at the end of the hall. Inside, a dozen technicians worked, surrounded by equipment and instruments and machines of all kinds. I could not help but wonder what may come if we were successful here today. By next summer, could the heart monitor beeping softly beside the single bed be married to the hot nurse checking a chart?

What we do here will change the winds, sowing the seed of

something uncertain, erasing antipathy and pollinating unpredictability.

"I'm scared," I said.

"I will still be me," Winston promised. "I will just look a little more like you."

"But no blue hair," I stated.

"No blue hair," Winston agreed.

They had mapped his mind over the course of many months. Every night, Winston logged on to an account and answered dozens of questions that determined his reaction to real world circumstances: "What would you do in the event of a natural disaster?" "Plumbs or prunes?" "What one word describes your world?" "What did you get for your tenth birthday?"

Weekly, he was subject to scans of his brainwaves. Powerful algorithms measured his emotional functions as he watched holograms of events to illicit random reactions. He was tired after those sessions, and fell asleep in my arms afterward.

Monthly, they spent an entire weekend in drills, creating real world scenarios in laboratory conditions that gauged his response to anything from being robbed at gunpoint to meeting a new friend to being lost at sea and left for dead. Winston was quiet for days after these monthly sessions. They were hardest. One month, he simply said, "I watched you die."

We waited two years. The waiting was over.

Winston reclined on the bed in the center of the room. Attendants applied monitors that transmitted vital signs and bioelectric metrics to screens surrounding us on all sides. Across the room was an empty space where Winston Price was going to be remade as something else.

"We're ready," Dr. Merriweather announced.

"I love you," I said, taking his hand.

"I love you," Winston replied, smiling.

Then it began.

Dr. Merriweather would take Winton out of his flesh and blood body and download my future husband into a Hard Light Construct. We wanted to prove to the lawmakers that banned us from ever marrying that the basis of soullessness was baseless. There is no soul. The essence of who we are is experience, instinct, inherent personality. We are the sparks and synopsis of a complex system. I am just as much a man as anyone made of bone and tissue.

We would prove love is not limited to spirit.

I let go of the hand. It was not Winston anymore. I walked over to the empty space. It started filling up with light and form. A HaLiCon formed before me with Winston's face, his same features and fashion and all his scars and imperfections. It was the same man, just glowing and ephemeral. His eyes were closed. What would I see when he opened them? Still Winston? Or something else?

I waited.

―――――――

Riley has never really fit in. Years spent at university were like lessons on how to be the same as everyone else, how to group-think, how to suppress differences and join the collective. Riley would never be like anyone else. Then Winston came along and the world changed. The things that always kept Riley apart from everyone made no difference to Winston. They fell in love. Now they enjoy midnight walks along the river and sitting along the shores staring up at the stars. But something still keeps them from being truly *together*.

―――――――

Eddie Newton was awarded the Robert L. Fish Memorial Award for the Best First American Mystery Short Story of the Year. His short story, "White," is presented in the anthology *Snowpocalypse*. He is the author of the political thriller e-novel, *American Herstory*. He lives in North Dakota with his wife Treina and his four children: Kobe, Gage, Oliver, and Bennett. He has never been called a mad scientist, although he did get really angry at a test tube once. And like most of us, he is still waiting...

LILY IN THE MOONLIGHT
An account by Professor Fia McCauley,
as told to Maureen Bowden

My namesake, Saint Fiacra, is the patron saint of gardeners, so I was destined to be a botanist. I specialised in lilies, the loveliest of flowers, but their beauty has too brief a life before it suffers, in Shakespeare's words, "The wrackful siege of battering days."

My life's work was to produce a hybrid lily possessing longevity. Obtaining seeds from the most long-lived species, I cross-pollinated again and again. The lilies didn't like it. Virginal by inclination, they prefer to reproduce asexually, by splitting their bulbs, allowing each segment to grow into a new plant. It was necessary, however, for me to subject them to the indignity of seeding, in order to achieve my goal.

I had friends in those early post-war days: former students from university, clinging to bizarre nicknames, hanging on to old relationships, before making their way in the world to find their niches, and leave me to mine. They visited me from time to time.

"What's the plan, Fi?" Jinks said. "Propagating man-eating plants to protect us against the next potential invader?"

"Don't be an ass," Bunty said, helping herself from my dish of assorted nuts and berries. "If Fi was doing that, the government wouldn't let her tell us. Do you want to be hanged as a spy?"

Corky picked up my mandolin. "Give us a burst on your banjo, Fi."

I forced myself to smile as I took it from him. "It's a mandolin, not a banjo."

"What's the difference?"

"A mandolin's more feminine."

I led them into the garden, where they were less intrusive, and I laughed at their lunacies until they left.

In time, the visits grew less frequent, then they stopped. I was happier without the distraction.

The last crop of lilies I'd grown from seed showed promising results. They were past their normal life span and still in full bloom. With each passing week, my optimism grew, but after six months, all but one started to fade. The survivor, with her pure white petals and crimson-tipped stigma, stood solitary and graceful: a perfect lily, surrounded by her wilted sisters.

I planted nothing more in the flowerbed. It was hers alone.

A compulsion to link our lives prompted me to dust her stamens for a sample of pollen. "My apologies, Lily," I said. "You'll not have to endure this again." I poured boiling water onto the sample, allowed it to cool, and drank it.

~

Forty years later, I still looked no older than twenty-five, and my Lily remained in bloom. She was my closest companion.

The college administrators had long forgotten me, but the current students still visited me for advice and encouragement. Kimberly, Cynthia, and Troy replaced Jinks, Bunty, and Corky.

"What do you think of Mrs Thatcher, Prof?" Kimberly asked.

"I don't understand, politics, Kim," I said. "Flowers are complicated enough for me."

"You like music, don't you, Prof?" Cynthia said. "I'll lend you the new Paul Simon album, *Graceland*. It's well crucial."

"You're very kind, Cyn, but I don't have anything to play it on. I make my own music."

Troy looked up from his copy of the *Radio Times*. "Have you seen the new Doctor Who, Prof? Sylvester McCoy. How gruesome is that?"

"Just for you, Troy, I'll set my man-eating plants on him."

They amused me, and I daresay I amused them, but I discouraged them from overstaying their welcome. I preferred to spend my time with Lily.

In the evening, I sat beside her flowerbed, playing my mandolin. I sang songs of my younger days: Bing Crosby's "When the Blue of the Night Meets the Gold of the Day," and "Beautiful Dreamer." I imagined Lily and I were harmonising with Bing and the Andrews Sisters as I sang, "Don't Fence Me In," "Is You Is Or Is You Ain't My Baby?" and, most fitting, "Magic is the Moonlight." She was at her loveliest by moonlight. It bathed her in a soft satin sheen. Before the need for sleep called me indoors, I sang "Goodnight Sweetheart," the late-night benediction that long ago, Al Bowley had crooned in London ballrooms while death's shadow stalked the land and the Luftwaffe did their worst overhead.

England in the latter half of the twentieth-century was a good time to be alive, and Lily and I were content. It was relatively peaceful, although, not so in other parts of the world, and nowhere can we long remain in isolation from the rest of humanity.

The twenty-first century brought a colder, more hostile dawn.

"The dogs of war are straining at the leash, my girl," I said. "Shadows are gathering again, but maybe you and I won't see them fall." We were long-lived, but not immortal.

I found a grey hair on my pillow when I awoke, one morning, and in the mirror I saw the signs of age around my eyes. My body's increasing frailty indicated that my decline would be swift, and I was not sorry.

Lily's head drooped a little lower these days, and her stigma's vibrancy was fading to pink. She was still beautiful, but she had mellowed. My instinct told me that it was time for her bulb to split. She would wilt, and her babies would blossom.

I visited the solicitors, Prys-Jones, Tudor-Jones, Parry-Jones and Assoc., to draw up my will.

Mr Tegwin Parry-Jones showed me into his office, "Coffee or tea, is it, Professor?"

"Coffee, please."

"Tidy." He pressed a button on his handset. "Bronwen, two coffees please. Quick as you like, isn't it?" He turned back to me. "She's my daughter. Helping out in the school holidays, see?"

I nodded, realising how much I'd stepped back from the human world, and I felt a momentary regret that I'd never had a daughter to help out in the school holidays. It soon passed. I'd made my choice, and I'd given Lily life. She would have daughters. For me, that was enough.

Mr Parry-Jones and I drank Bronwen's coffee and I gave him his instructions. "I want to leave all my property to the horticultural college," I said, "on condition that they maintain my gardens. I'm naming you as my executor and trustee, and I expect you to make sure that they do."

"What's occurrin' as to your funeral, Professor?" This Welshman didn't mince his words.

"I wish to be cremated and my ashes raked into my empty flower bed. There will already be bulbs in the soil. Nothing else is to be planted."

My bones would nourish the earth where Lily's babies would grow.

At moonrise, I took my mandolin and a garden chair to Lily's flowerbed, and I sat beside her. "You're looking good, Lil," I said.

"So are you, Fi."

I didn't hear her say that, of course. I may be eccentric, but I'm not barking mad, yet the tilt of her head in the night breeze told me that she would have said it if she could. I sang to her, one last time: words I'd set to "Lily Marlene," a wartime favourite.

"Together in the garden, we greet the midnight hour,
age-old companions, a woman and a flower.
Time comes upon us, as it must,
soon we'll crumble into dust:
my Lily in the moonlight,
my Lily and my life."

Footnote:

"The wrackful siege of battering days" (William Shakespeare, Sonnet no.65, Line 6.)

———

Professor Fia McCauley was born in 1920. She studied at the Northern England University College of Horticulture, making a valuable contribution to the development of farming practices and food production throughout World War II. She obtained a PhD, and when the war ended, she purchased a smallholding from university land and turned her attention to botany. She died in 2016, bequeathing her estate back to the university. The students still tend her flowers.

———

Maureen Bowden is a Liverpudlian living with her musician husband in North Wales. She has had eighty-four stories and poems accepted for publication by paying markets. Silver Pen publishers nominated one of her stories for the 2015 international Pushcart Prize. She also writes song lyrics, mostly comic political satire, set to traditional melodies. Her husband has performed these in Folk clubs throughout England and Wales. She loves her family and friends, Rock 'n' Roll, Shakespeare, and cats.

INTRODUCTION TO THE EPIC OF
CENTIPIDUS
An essay by Edward Mathis, as provided by Hamilton Perez

You were likely drawn to *The Epic of Centipidus* by one of two factors. The first is the legend itself: full of mystery, intrigue, adventure, and war, taking place on the smallest grand theater a story can be set. Whether it be the pill bugs rolled down mole-hills, crushing enemies in their path; or the labyrinthine, cavernous abode of the ants which no traveler can escape without the aid of the capricious Queen; or the taciturn hero, who famously has "more legs than words at his disposal," it's no wonder the epic has been described as "the Iliad of insects."[1]

I suspect, however, that what brought you was not the wonder of the tale, but the second factor, which has received far more attention.

It began with my insistence that I be listed as the book's translator, rather than its author. This, of course, begged the question: *Who wrote it?* and my answer has turned friends and colleagues against me, but it also inspired a trend of searching uncut lawns for strange glyphs written on grass leaves.

As academics debated the issue, the media largely lampooned it. Fox News did a roundtable discussion which cast the unlikely spotlight on "experts" in the field. Forget Joe the Plumber—Terry the Exterminator is here to tell you there are no bug languages, bug cultures, or bug books.

The Nightly Show did a skit in which Larry Wilmore interviewed a

---

[1] Anthony Gallego. "A Bug's Lie." *Time* Mar. 2016: 64. Print.

giant grasshopper in Groucho Marx disguise. The conspicuously named Hugh Mann claimed to be an entomologist and assured us that there is no secret insect society, and we should all just go about our lives grazing grasslands and raising pupae.[2]

Despite the evidence included in the appendices, skeptics have persisted in painting me as a puppet master pulling strings in an elaborate and theatrical hoax. But it was never my ambition to inspire the budding field of cultural entomology. That was something passed on to me by my father, and I think it cost him his life.

~

The last I ever heard from him was a strange voicemail he left me. He'd found something unusual on his Missouri acreage, something he couldn't make sense of. "If you look closely—" The message cut off.

When I tried getting hold of him, my calls just went to the answering machine. Dad refused to own a cell phone, let alone carry one, so at first I didn't worry. But after a few days without word, I grew concerned. He was all alone out there; meanwhile, I was deconstructing texts half a country away.

Three days after that first message, the phone rang. I rushed to answer it, and on the other end, the compassionate but no less official voice of Seligman P.D. asked if I was Gregory Mathis, Dad's next of kin.

The tinny voice informed me that a neighbor found him in his home, sprawled across the kitchen floor after an apparent stroke.

All sorts of things ran through my head then—none of them what should have: "If you look closely—"

It didn't occur to me that there might be a connection between his final message and his death. Not until after I returned to my old home and saw the strange glyphs he'd been drawing, the leaf-litter scattered through his office, did the uneasy sense of foul play first creep into my mind.

---

[2] Of course, insects don't actually rear their young. One can't help feeling the joke would have landed better if a little more research had been put in beforehand.

44

~

Returning to my childhood home was an eerie experience. An empty house is disturbingly corpse-like, possessing all the appearance of life, though a chilling stillness whispers otherwise.

Dad and I used to sit on the porch, watching the sun bruise the clouds deep purples and reds, listening as the air became electric with the chattering buzz of insects. This ritual I now undertook alone, and the empty chair beside me ached like a phantom limb.

But then I noticed something unusual nearby. At the lip of the field, a cricket was perched on a blade of grass, scratching its legs together as if to sing but making no sound.[3]

What appeared to mute the cricket was a blade of grass caught between its legs. Intending only to move the insect, my approaching hand scared it off entirely. The night might have ended there, and the world might have been the happier, but the grass leaf which the cricket had been standing on now caught my attention.

There were markings on it that seemed like more than just arbitrary scratches. They had the look—the *feel*—of intention. And there was something achingly familiar about them as well.

I took the grass leaf inside and examined it with a magnifying glass from my father's study. That's when I recognized where I'd seen this mark before. It matched one of the many symbols that Dad had drawn.

The implication was certainly absurd, and I spent the rest of the night determined to prove the absurd idea wrong. I stalked through fields of long, uncut grass, searching for leaves with unusual markings on them.

I found an astonishing number.

Each was brought inside to be carefully analyzed under a light and magnifying glass, and after comparing a hundred or so to the first and finding no discernible system, I had nearly given up. But then I examined one that matched the first perfectly, as if made by a copyist.

Looking over the others, I started noticing patterns and

---

[3] At this point, I was still under the misconception that crickets chirp by rubbing their legs together. They actually produce sound by scraping their wings.

consistencies—a clearly organized system of communication. I could hardly believe it. I'd stumbled upon the writings of an insect language.

~

"If you look closely—"
This was what my father had discovered, and it was possibly the greatest discovery since heliocentrism—that we are not alone in the universe. In fact, we have never been alone, and all this time we've been looking to the stars we ought to have been looking to our toes.

It felt as though he had dropped his torch before passing, and I'd returned home to find it still blazing—to carry it in his stead. In a way, I felt closer to him than I had in all the years separated by state lines.

Initially, I suspected this language to be rudimentary, only capable of conveying simple concepts like "Water nearby" or "Danger." It couldn't be too difficult to decipher, I thought. I had no idea the tremendous feat I was undertaking.

Dad's study became my workroom. Bookshelves were cleared to make room for catalogs of data. The walls were plastered with high resolution photographs, and the desk was buried under books exploring language, ciphers, and insect behavior.

Translating started as a game but developed into something more important as comprehension continually eluded me. As I studied the texts from different angles, I found the writings more and more complex.

I was not deterred, however. I was obsessed.

Days burned away, squinting and scribbling. I missed Dad's funeral, only realizing a full week after he'd been buried. My sabbatical from grad school passed in a flurry. Emails and phones calls went unanswered. I couldn't leave. This was too important. What could be greater?

Experimenting with different methods of translation proved fruitless though. The texts before me seemed just as alien. I needed help.

I captured a cricket and placed it in a square-shaped jar with three common phrases drawn on small pieces of paper and taped to the walls, facing inward. A blank grass leaf was provided for the cricket to write upon.

The cricket examined the writing on the walls, curiously. When it turned toward me, I wrote another phrase and showed it to the cricket. It was unimpressed. I wrote another. Once again the cricket was unresponsive. Finally, I taped a fresh Germander flower to the last open wall of the jar and left for the night.

My expectations for what the cricket might write were as numerous as a black widow's brood. Would the cricket describe the blue color? Would it identify the flower by its genus and species? Would it simply write: "flower"?

The next day there was a marking on the grass leaf. I had no way to read the note, but it was nonetheless a promising step forward. I only learned much later what was written was actually an insect phrase for "Leave me the hell alone."

I bought over a hundred jars and spent long nights collecting crickets in the field. I decided to stick with the same insect for consistency. After all, I'd only seen a cricket make these markings. Perhaps they were the only ones that did—an insect *intelligentsia*.[4]

Using photographs for translations proved the most useful technique for learning other parts of speech. A picture of a toad would be placed side by side with a picture of a toad jumping. Similarly, a picture of a dog might be contrasted with that of a wet dog—or a dead dog.

It was important to keep the crickets content, and not merely captives. They were never kept in jars for long periods. Once they etched their markings, they were transferred to a large terrarium designed to mimic their natural habitat, including an attached room with moist substrate for breeding.

This brings me to one obvious challenge to be overcome in human-bug relations, and that is the dramatic contrast in longevity. Thousands of crickets were born and died during the course of the experiment. To view them each as individuals would keep one in a perennial state of grief. To give them each their own grave would quickly crowd the field with tiny tombstones.

---

[4] Further study has revealed that, just as in the human world, there are many different languages as well as dialects. The world of arthropods, however, has evolved to be far more multicultural than our own. A cricket might speak its own native language as well as that of flies, centipedes, earwigs, and mosquitoes.

Instead, I created a mass grave site with one large stone beside it to commemorate their lives and their contribution to my research.

The crickets certainly weren't viewed as friends. Nor did I treat them as "people," as one might find it tempting to anthropomorphize them like dogs. There was respect, but never camaraderie. I never learned any of their names, nor they, mine.

That was until I met Crickthus.[5]

In order to keep incoming generations literate and in touch with their cultural heritage, it was necessary to periodically introduce crickets from the fields into the terrarium. When I first spotted Crickthus, I mistook him for a cockroach, so large was he and so dark his coat. But he was clearly writing, perched atop a thick blade of grass.

I put him in a small terrarium used to initiate newcomers before integrating them with the others. This terrarium included leaves to write upon and a note taped to one of the walls that explained the enterprise they were now a part of.

Most captives left notes requesting that I let them go, or not kill them, or—by far the most common—that if I told their mating partners they put up a valiant fight but were tragically squished and shouldn't be looked for, they would cooperate entirely.[6]

Crickthus simply wrote: "You're in way over your head," followed by a curious sign that I spent hours failing to decipher. Only through asking him, days later, did I learn that this curious scratch and scribble was his signature.

During our first sessions, he lectured me through a series of notes, chastising me for interrupting his endless work cataloguing manuscripts. I had to continuously drop in more leaves for him to write on. Crickthus came around only after learning of my grand enterprise, and was henceforth delighted to discover someone interested in learning about his culture.

---

[5] Names of insects are rough, phonetic approximations. Insect languages consist mostly of chirps, clicks, and hisses.

[6] While insects have no official form of marriage, monogamy is the closest analogue that functions as a social institution. Unfortunately, insects are even less evolved for this than humans and have a persistent, itching need to escape from it shortly after entering.

As it turns out, most insects aren't inclined to read for pleasure. Crickthus was an exception. He was a scholar, an educator of sorts.

He was quite critical at first, pointing out that all the texts I'd been translating were writing exercises used for educating. If crickets had a kindergarten, my manuscripts would be their "Letters to Mom."

With his direction, I discovered the monistic philosophy of Betlen, the 18th century beetle;[7] the romances of Lady Arget, the 12th century lady bug; and the tragicomedies of the contemporary cockroach Barmalowe—my favorite being the story of Icthyl, the suicidal cockroach who repeatedly fails at killing himself: "I will die if it's the last thing I do!"[8]

A whole new world opened up to me, a world of adventure and intrigue occurring in the most mundane, unexceptional places. My bedroom or my kitchen might be the setting of some harrowing adventure or sweeping epic. The battle of good and evil occurs not just at Armageddon, nor the hearts of human beings, but also in our cupboards, our backyard gardens, our basements, and our bed sheets.

Indeed, there is much we can learn from the tragically short but nevertheless full and fulfilled lives of insects. Their world is so vast, so beautiful, so new, so full of wonder. "All is not illusion," writes Betlen, dismissing the coleopteran skeptics that *anything* exists. "All is imagination!"[9]

Many of the works I was translating were too long for a single blade of grass, or even a large leaf. *The Epic of Centipidus* consisted

---

[7] Insects have no exact concept of centuries; in fact, they have no real thought of years. Most only think of time by hours, days, or at most weeks. The work of a termite historian proved exceptionally helpful. He used seasons to chronicle long periods of time, charting migrations of certain other insects and predatory birds. Using this and certain references to plagues and natural disasters, for instance the Lisbon earthquake of 1755, I have calculated when many of these writers likely lived. I have included my calculations in Appendix D in the back of the book.

[8] *The Life and Death of Icthyl* III, ii, 58

[9] Betlen. *Eyes and Legs of Gods*. New York, NY: Stone & Benn, 2015. 203. Print.

of over two-hundred grass leaves that would have taken weeks of dedicated work to get in the proper order without his help.

My relationship with Crickthus inspired a dramatic change in my treatment of insects and other arthropods. How many times had I swatted at, even hunted, an irritating fly? How often had I called the exterminator? How many newspapers and shoes had I wielded like a weapon?

And the literature itself! Imagine the countless stories and philosophies potentially lost forever every time somebody mowed their lawn.

It comes as no surprise that humans have something of an unfriendly reputation amongst insects (even more so with arachnids),[10] which will have to be overcome if our two civilizations are to merge.

To make amends, I began bleeding myself after dinner and leaving droplets of blood on the backdoor stoop for the mosquitoes. Spiders traversed the walls of the house with impunity. Ants found leftovers in a great pile outside.

In retrospect, this may have drawn too much attention.

One afternoon, I went to collect the latest translations and found the crickets, each in their individual jars, hopping about like lunatics. They were chirping and hitting the glass with their bodies, making an awful cacophony of shrill notes and soft thuds. Each demanded my immediate attention except for one which was strangely inactive. Leaning closer I realized, to my horror, its head was missing. It was *murdered*.

The crickets wouldn't tell me what happened; they refused to speak. Even Crickthus was unresponsive. This was more disturbing than the homicide itself. To have my friend and mentor suddenly revert to such a state of non-identity shook me.

I buried the decapitated body at the grave site and determined to forget the incident. It was a fluke. An accident. Something that could be prevented with stricter security measures.

One can only deny the truth for so long before it comes skittering out from behind the dresser and crawling up your leg.

---

[10] There is a famous arachnid tale of revenge—akin to our *Count of Monte Cristo*—in which a noble, impoverished spider is unjustly swatted at by a human only to escape and return for revenge once the would-be assassin is sleeping.

That night there was a cricket head waiting on my pillow. I was being warned.

I kept at my work developing the Cricket-English Dictionary and translating various texts. The crickets remained unresponsive. Many wouldn't even look at me. Crickthus gave me nothing.

Setting twelve jars in a row with a cricket and a leaf in each, I wrote a note asking why they had stopped working and assuring that I could protect them. Hours passed before one of the twelve wrote something down. It was Crickthus.

The others hopped about violently. I opened the jar and retrieved the note. The message read, "They're coming for us."

Who were *they*? And who was *us*? Did us mean only the crickets, or was I included as well? The solitude that I'd experienced during the crickets' silence was now reversed. Now I felt nothing but eyes on me—unblinking eyes hiding in every corner, watching, waiting.

In a panic, I left the house. There was no where I could escape to, though. No one I could call. Who could I turn to? Who could protect me? Who could make it alright?

Only then, in my helpless, fearful state, did I realize that it had been three years since the enterprise began. Three years holed up in my father's house with minimal human contact. Three years a hermit scribbling secrets to crickets.

There was only ever one person I could always rely on.

~

They misspelled his name. "Arther Mathis" read Dad's tombstone, and I knew then how badly I'd let him down.

Dad always said it's the little things in life that are most important. They're the easiest things to miss, but they're what make the difference. "Pay attention to what's in front of you," he used to say. "And underneath."

Were *they* what killed him?

"If you look closely—"

I tried telling him about my research, about what I'd found. I tried to unburden myself to him as though he were alive, telling him about our discovery and the awful things now resulting from it. But talking to a headstone is a lot like prayer: trying to get a reaction from a wall. It just stares back at you, stone-faced and cold.

All I could imagine was his stern countenance, glaring at me for abandoning the crickets in a fit of fear. Then a monarch butterfly landed on his gravestone and rested there, observing me. It waved its antennae my direction.

Another landed beside the first. And another. There was one on my wrist, two on my shoulder. Soon the whole cemetery was swarming orange and black, fire and smoke.

My heart sank. While butterflies are often symbols of hope and change in our culture, they foreshadow catastrophe and doom in the literature of bugs.[11]

I raced back to the house, and when I returned, I found one of the jars was now full of webbing. A cricket head, body, and six legs were severed and spaced apart on the web in a grotesque anatomical display.

As I approached, I could tell by the size and the dark color of the individual that this was not just any cricket—it was my friend. It was Crickthus. In my terror, I'd forgotten to put the lid back on.

The rest of the crickets were catatonic, mere shells. I realized too late: they were being silenced.

~

There was a strong desire to give Crickthus a private grave, one as large as his influence was in my life, one that would draw more notice than the mass grave I'd given to all those that came before and all those that would follow.

I knew it wasn't right, though. The others were just as much individuals as Crickthus. To single him out would be to deny their identities, almost their existence, and so I buried him with the rest, though this was the first burial that drew tears.

That night when I went to bed, I found a brown recluse hiding under my sheets. It seemed to be waiting for me. I realized then that my persecutors didn't want to create a union between humans and arthropods and would do anything to prevent it. My assailant escaped before I could squash him.

In the morning, I went to the nearest general store and returned home with a can of Raid holstered to my belt and my pant legs tucked into my socks. I brought the cricket terrarium into my room

---

[11] Hence the phrase: "Never trust a Monarch Butterfly."

and duct taped the windowsills and door frames around the house.

The threats only got worse, however.

Once, I awoke to find hundreds of cricket corpses in my bed; the enemy had raided the grave site.

The worst was when, in the middle of translating at my desk, a horde of black widows crawled up my legs. I sprayed them with pesticide and jumped out of my clothes and nearly out of my skin. I put their bodies on toothpicks and placed them at the windows and doors as warnings to the others.

I could no longer protect the crickets; I could barely protect myself. The crickets remained unresponsive. I had no more use for them, and keeping them in the house only endangered them further. I freed them a mile away from the house.

Walking away from my former colleagues was painful. I had emptied the terrarium gently into the grass, and the crickets sat there, lifeless. I stood over them, pleading internally for them to move, to escape, to be free.

At last, one of them leapt and disappeared into the wild. Another rode on a friend's back. A pair strolled off together atop intersecting grass leaves, following some path only they recognized.

At home, I could hear my prosecutors in the walls. I couldn't understand them, of course, but I distinctly recognized the hushed hisses, clicks, and gargles of insect speech. I could hear the buzzing of wings and tap of hard bodies bouncing off each other.

There was some sort of parliament going on, I'm sure of it.

Over the next few days I could hear them almost constantly, to the point that I suspected—*still suspect*—they were following me throughout the house.

Initially, I wondered if they were studying me as I was studying them. There was something far more sinister going on, however.

They became all the louder when I tried to sleep. Some of them climbed in my bed, bit and pinched and itched me terribly. Spiders and ants and earwigs, all crawling under my sheets. I couldn't shut my eyes without feeling the tickle of some foreign creature on my body and the nervous need to scratch all over.

Before long, I was attacking the walls of my home with a sledgehammer, and the creatures must have anticipated this, for as soon as I swung through the wall they were nowhere to be found.

I was no longer master of the house. The insidious insects had found their way in and were driving me out. The long battle was lost before I knew it began.

The house that my father had passed on to me was difficult to leave, but it had become something different than the home I grew up in, even different than the home I began my life's work in. It was full of memories beautiful and pure, but also painful and hard. To preserve the good, I poured gasoline on the walls and floorboards and lit the house like a funeral pyre.

~

Arthropods, it turns out, are neither quick to forgive, nor to forget. Their connecting webs span the length of cities, states, perhaps even countries.

I find traces of them everywhere: small holes puncturing the pages of notebooks, leaving them illegible; spider webs in my hair when I wake up; dead crickets scattered throughout the house. I have yet to spot a living one.

Whether it is their intention, I cannot say, but the critics and insects are working in tandem to prevent the merge. The arthropods sought to drive me insane, and the critics want to prove they've done their job.

I hope that you, reader, haven't been dissuaded by my prosecutors. There are forces at work all around us that we cannot see nor comprehend. The simplest answer isn't usually the right one; it almost never is. But it satisfies our nagging curiosity. We are creatures that can bear anything but the thought of not knowing. That's why we bother with belief.

It may be, however, that my critics will not be silenced until I am. Once they find my body drained of blood by mosquitoes, or swollen with bites and stings, or covered in a crawling, writhing, all-consuming blackness of ants—then they'll know. They'll understand. It was all true after all.

Again, it is the little things that are the most dangerous. And there are an awful lot of little things.

Edward Mathis
Berkeley, California
March 2016

Editor's Note: Edward Mathis was reported missing four days after submitting this introduction. Authorities are following several leads regarding his whereabouts.

Edward Mathis is a cultural entomologist, lecturer, and the acclaimed translator of many controversial texts including *Seven-Legged Spider*, *Stone and Carapace*, and *The Life and Death of Icthyl*.

Hamilton Perez is a writer and freelance editor living in Sacramento, California. He enjoys long walks through the woods and things that aren't real. His stories have also appeared in *Daily Science Fiction* and *Between Worlds*.

THE FISSURE OF ROLANDO
An essay by Euphemia Thorniwork,
as provided by Judith Field

A splash of water in my face brought me round. I opened my eyes and sat up to find myself in the lecture theatre of Huxley College, Oxford, where a mathematics lecture was in progress. Spaulding, my fellow student, knelt at my side with knitted brows, an empty glass in his hand.

"Are you alright, Euphemia?" he whispered. "You fainted and slid from your seat to the floor. I took it upon myself to apply first aid. Do you require more water?"

"No!" I dragged myself back into my seat and pulled my handkerchief out of my cuff to dry my face. "No, thank you. I am quite myself."

Spaulding took his place and looked toward the blackboard at the front of the hall. There were mutterings from several parts of the audience about feeble women who were simply not up to the job. Dr Wagstaff continued his lecture as though he had not noticed my faint.

The dim lamps in the hall matched the gloom I felt. I groaned inwardly, cursing myself for swooning like a character from a melodrama. Shifting in my seat, I was unable to get comfortable or concentrate. I jumped as Dr Wagstaff banged the chalk down onto the table in front of him to make a point I had not heard. The chalk shattered into a cloud of dust, which settled on his whiskers, changing them from grey, to white.

The letter from my mother was the cause of my loss of consciousness. It arrived just as I was leaving for College, and I made the mistake of opening it during the lecture. She told me that Barings were virtually insolvent following imprudent investments in the Argentine. I had lost most of my legacy from Uncle Eric. There was enough to last until the end of this term. Four weeks, and then my time as the first female student of mathematics at Huxley College would be at an end. I began to feel dizzy again and rummaged in my Gladstone bag for smelling salts but found none.

I pushed the letter inside the bag, next to one Mother had sent me earlier in the week, informing me that Mr. Driver who owned the pharmacy had been enquiring after me again. She considered that he would ask me to walk out with him next time I was at home. My stomach turned at the thought of keeping company with sweaty-faced Thomas Driver and his hot breath that smelled of fish. But unless I could fund my continuing academic career, penury would force me to do so, with him or someone like him. If I were a man, I could find gainful employment. But for me, it was a choice between Driver, or scratching an existence as a spinster, invisible without a man by my side.

I had to find a source of income. I poked and prodded inside the bag again, but other than my keys and the two letters from Mother, all it contained was the classified advertisement I had torn out of the newspaper:

Wanted immediately at the home of a gentleman scholar a prudent, steady and careful assistant without dependents for novel physics research project of vital importance and of the utmost confidentiality. Each evening, all day Saturday and Sunday. Must be accustomed to the maintenance of glass instruments and equipment and to working with the electrophorus and the dry cell. Good character indispensible. Ability to hold breath for at least one minute a distinct advantage. Five shillings per week offered. Apply to Dr Q Wagstaff at the office of this paper.

I had not been surprised to see it, for the college was rife with rumours about Dr Wagstaff. It was said that he had already had three assistants this term, one after the other, and they had never been seen again. Had they simply been too embarrassed to show their faces? I had been intrigued, but not brave enough to reply. Nor had the need existed—then. Desperation made me consider seeking this post, despite it paying the wages of a parlourmaid. At the end of the lecture, I waited until all the other students left, hoping that the post was still vacant. I walked on shaking legs down to the front of the theatre and spoke to him.

~

At almost 9 o'clock on Saturday morning, I trudged through the rain along the street leading to Dr Wagstaff's house. A bicycle bell rang behind me. Before I could move aside, a man on a velocipede rattled past me across the cobblestones through a puddle. Muddy water spattered onto my skirt, making the hem droop in damp folds round my ankles.

I stood on Dr Wagstaff's doorstep and tugged the bell pull. A woman I estimated to be in her sixties opened the door, coughing and wafting her hand in front of her face. Behind her, green vapour filled the hall to about knee height. The smell of burnt hair hit the back of my throat.

"Kindly tell your master that Miss Thorniwork is here," I gulped as I tried to peer round her.

"Never heard of you. Get along, now." The rain dripped onto my head from a leaky gutter. She eyed me up and down. I must have made a poor specimen but I drew myself up to my full height of five feet three and three quarter inches and tried to look her in the eye.

"Dr Wagstaff instructed me to attend here at 9 o'clock, precisely."

"Here to see the Doctor? Not on your life. The very idea! Enough to make a stuffed bird laugh."

"Do not waste my time. See, here." I pulled the remains of the page bearing the advertisement out of my pocket and showed it to her.

She waved it away. "Go along with you. Drat your insolence."

"Enquire of Dr Wagstaff. He will confirm the appointment."

"I will do no such thing. If you don't take yourself off, and precious sharp, I'll go and fetch the police." She moved as though to shut the door in my face.

A future in a marriage breeding cannon fodder for the Empire loomed in my mind. I felt my hands shake. I spoke again, my mouth dry.

"Has there never been an occasion when an unannounced visitor arrived to see the Doctor? Please. Just ask him. Then if he denies all knowledge, I swear I will leave."

"Hmm." Her mouth set in a line. She took up a speaking tube

from the wall inside the doorway, pulled a brass cover from the end and blew into it. A whistle sounded. I heard a faint voice from the other end: "Yes, Mrs Howell?"

"A young lady. *Unaccompanied.*" She put the cap back onto the tube and stood, hands on hips.

I peered past her again. Dr Wagstaff appeared through a door at the end of the hall. He strode toward her, his wrinkled face wreathed in smiles. "Thank you, Mrs Howell, the young lady is expected. I apologise for my lack of prior announcement."

She glared her disapproval and stepped aside.

Dr Wagstaff rubbed his hands together. "Capital," he said, looking downward. "Ah, I see the rolandic vapour is settling. Therefore, it is, as I hoped, heavier than air."

Mrs Howell dabbed at her watering eyes with the corner of her apron. "Enough to give me the green sickness. I hope you have lost your sense of smell, *Miss.*" She sniffed, turned and went inside the house.

Dr Wagstaff turned to me. "I fear I have annoyed Mrs Howell by covering the carpet with green gas again," he said. "But I am forgetting my manners, leaving you standing on the doorstep. Please come in."

I hung my hat and coat on a peg and put my umbrella in a hollowed out elephant's foot that already contained a furled parasol with a brass duck's head for a handle, a gnarled wooden walking stick with a solar topi dangling from a protrusion on the end, and what might have been a rapier from the look of the haft. He led me along a wide hallway past dark wooden doors till we came to one that was half open, leading into the scullery.

Dr Wagstaff stopped next to a scrubbed wooden table in the middle of the room. "First, I must ask you to sign this agreement." He reached into a jacket pocket and extracted a creased piece of paper and a fountain pen.

"Allow me to read it first." I took the paper from him, unfolded it and put it down on the table. "Keep secret all I see, hear and do. Of course." I ran my finger down the page as I read, stopping at an unfamiliar word. "What does this mean—'accept the risk of transmigration and/or transmutation'"?

"A mere formality. Do not concern yourself."

I read on. "And ... 'confirm that my spine is flexible and has suffered no previous injury'"?

"Surely a young person such as you need not be concerned with that." He waved the pen under my nose.

"Agree that my estate and relicts have no claim on you? Perhaps I should ask a solicitor to examine this document."

Dr Wagstaff pursed his lips and tapped his chin with the pen. "Such timidity does you no credit, Miss Thorniwork. Without boldness, there can be no advancement. You must ask yourself whether you want this post at all. Indeed, I may reconsider my offer of employment."

I thought of Mother's letter yet again, snatched the pen, and scrawled my name at the end of the paper. Dr Wagstaff took the pen from me and placed his signature beneath mine.

"This way." He walked to the far end of the scullery and opened another door. Tendrils of the same green mist snaked out. "Welcome to my laboratory. Please hold your breath!" I breathed in as deeply as I could. Just inside the doorway, through the green clouds, I saw a stuffed swordfish dangling from the ceiling.

"Ah, mind your head, Miss Thorniwork. Once the vapour— quite harmless, I assure you—disperses, you will see more clearly."

I rubbed my left temple. He bowed, and ushered me inside. I exhaled in a rasp.

"Breath held for twenty seconds," he muttered to himself. "That must suffice." He looked up at the fish. "My first attempt at taxidermy."

It reminded me of something similar in a painting I had seen, called "The Alchemist at Work." Or had that shown a suspended crocodile?

"I needed the bony bill of the fish for the experiment you are to help me with," he said. "It involves electricity."

"In fish?"

He shook his head and frowned. "I needed a conductor of electricity, but metal would not do. The part of a bone that is compressed will become negatively charged, while the part of the same bone that is under tension will become positively charged."

"If you say so. I am a mathematics student with little knowledge of physics." I felt my face grow warm, and I bit my lip, hoping that I had not just terminated my employment. "But I do find that elliptical geometry and ... Riemann's Hypothesis hold a curious fascination. What would you like me to do?" I said, with an artificial smile.

"I have heard great things about your tenacity and your inquiring mind. And you will help me in the development of mathematical methods that can be applied to problems in physics. I have observed your diligence during my lectures, the probing and incisive nature of the questions you ask. I will trust you with my discovery."

He shut the door behind us. Gas lamps flickered and cast long shadows. Dr Wagstaff turned a regulator on the wall and the lamps shone brighter. The walls were bare brickwork, painted white, as was the floor. There was a window made of reinforced glass that was either frosted or filthy—I did not care to find out which. Dark wooden shelves held jars filled with liquids in a range of colours I had not thought existed: blues so bright they seemed to etch the back of my eyes so that saw them behind my eyelids when I blinked. At the bottom of a carboy filled with purple liquid that fluoresced yellow round the edges was a blackened object. I looked closer. Could it be a minuscule brain?

I gasped. "From a rat?"

"I doubt Mrs Howell would thank you for that judgment on the last of her pickled walnuts. Would you like it?" He rummaged through his jacket pockets. "I have a fork somewhere."

I shuddered and shook my head.

He shrugged his shoulders. "Not hungry? No matter. Now come along." He hurried toward the end of the room.

As I passed a bench, movement in a jar the size of my head, filled with bright orange fluid, caught my eye, and I stopped to look. An oily globule the size of a hen's egg rose to the top of the liquid, floated for a moment, then fell back to the bottom like lava. I walked past racks of shelving lining the walls, laden with heaps of contorted glass tubing and vessels that seemed to have been twisted into sailor knots. At the opposite end of the room, next to a low stone sink, stood a bench on which stood a pair of metal rods mounted on a dais shaped like a squat cylinder. The rods inclined away from each other in a v-shape and a spark crackled from side to side between them. A smell of ozone replaced the smell of burnt hair.

A japanned screen, inlaid with a marquetry image of a slice of human brain in side view concealed one corner of the room from view.

"What I want your help with is over here." Dr Wagstaff moved the screen aside, revealing Regency-style chairs surrounding a card table covered in green baize. In the middle of it stood a mahogany box about one foot square and six inches high. On top of one side was a wooden shape like a pyramid with the top sliced away, inlaid with engraved brass plates. Some of these bore dials, some levers, still others apparently purely decorative. In the place of the point of the pyramid was an upright glass cylinder the length of my arm and twice the width, filled with clear liquid and capped with silver-coloured metal at both ends. Metallic probes projected into the cylinder from the caps. A copper cable as thick as my thumb ran from the top down to a smaller box on which were mounted two fluted glass bell-shaped devices resembling gas lamp shades but facing forward, one pointing to the left and one to the right.

We sat down at opposite sides of the table. He cleared his throat. "You see before you a device that will revolutionise communication within buildings. No longer will the master of a house have to ring for a servant. An employer will be able to speak to his staff without rising from his place to blow down a tube, as I do when I wish to speak to Mrs Howell. But, most excitingly, those whom illness has deprived of speech will be able to engage in dialogue."

I saw no wires. "Is it similar to Mr Bell's device? I have heard that he has developed an electric telephone that will transmit over a few feet."

He shook his head. "Speech is not required. It employs the electrical impulses that are generated in the brain." He pointed at the picture of the brain cross-section on the screen. "Now, when we intend to speak, before we do so, electric currents are generated. I have found a previously undiscovered function of part of the brain. Contrary to what the self-styled experts of the day would have us believe, the electric currents do not merely dissipate." He jumped to his feet, put his finger to his lips, crept to the door, and jerked it open. There was nobody there. "I have already demonstrated that this knowledge can be dangerous, if not treated with respect." I called to mind the rumours about the previous assistants. "It could have catastrophic results, in the wrong hands." He sprinted to the diagram and jabbed at a deep crevasse shown at the top of the brain. "Once generated, the currents remain. They are stored here, in a part of the brain the name of which I dare not speak, lest it be overheard." From his pocket he pulled out the stub of a pencil, and a scrap of crumpled paper. He scribbled something and handed the paper to me.

On it he had written "The Fissure of Rolando." It sounded like the title of one of mother's gothic novels. "You have read what I wrote?" I nodded, and he snatched the paper from my fingers and tore it into pieces. These he dropped onto the brickwork floor. He retrieved a box of matches from his jacket pocket and set them alight. "Catastrophic," he muttered, grinding the charred remains to powder under his heel.

He returned to my side of the screen and took a box from one of the shelves on the wall behind him. "This headgear is an integral part of the mechanism." From the box he took a black rubber, close-fitting cap which he tugged onto his head. It had a large round hole on each side through which he pulled his ears. He fastened an elasticated strap under his chin. "This ensures that the cap comes into close contact with the head and picks up the electrical impulses."

From the cap protruded rows of small round studs, from each of which a wire led. They collected at the back in the manner of a horse's tail about a yard long, at the end of which was a thick metal pin. This he plugged into a hole on the side of the cut-down pyramid.

"And now, yours." He took a similar cap out of the box and handed it to me.

I stretched it over my bun, eased my ears out and fastened the chin strap. It tugged at my hair. I felt my head perspire.

"Now, to test it." Dr Wagstaff plugged in the wires extending from the cap on my head. "I am thinking of a word. The energy from my brain collects in the rolandic tube here," he pointed at the glass cylinder. The fluid inside changed from clear to apple green and bubbles appeared at the probes at each end. "The colour changes and bubbles indicate an accumulation of charge. Eventually the electrons are discharged at the cathode on the top. The movement of electrons—an electrical current, you know—is transmitted down this cable, which is in fact the swordfish bill, coated with copper. And when the message is transmitted to you, notes sound for confirmation, amplified by these two glass bells."

Two notes chimed from the machine, and I had the curious sensation of Dr Wagstaff's voice inside my head. The liquid inside the tube changed back to clear. "Now, you please think of a word."

I did so, and the process repeated itself. We removed our caps and unplugged them from the machine. Damp tendrils of hair fell down around my face and I pushed them back behind my ears.

"You thought 'swordfish'," I said, dabbing at my forehead with my handkerchief.

"I did. And you, 'Barings'. A lot of fools." He tutted and shook his head.

"So, we know that it works," I said. "But, both parties must be connected to it. And, although one could use long cables to do so ... most impractical."

"Certainly, for all but the immobile. I seek your help to develop a wireless version. Electric waves move through space at the speed of light, as Maxwell has demonstrated. But we need to boost the sensitivity of the rolandic cylinder if we are to collect them." He took a grey, cylindrical object about a foot high and three inches across, with two metal pieces on the top, from a shelf beside the window.

"Now I will connect this dry cell via the relay, which will boost the current further." He wound a piece of wire round a metal stud protruding from the end of the cylinder. "I must be careful not to loosen the end terminal or the fluid escapes as vapour. I did so earlier, to Mrs Howell's indignation, and you walked through the results. Should that happen, you would do well to hold your breath. Now I shall think of another word."

The fluid changed colour, this time to a dark bottle green and bubbles appeared, but I heard no sound in my head and no chiming tone. A crackle came from the glass bells.

"I am detecting an unusual wave pattern." Dr Wagstaff stared at one of the dials on the machine. The needle on the instrument flicked to the left and then the right, left and right, in time with a new two-tone sound coming from the bells. The thud of a heartbeat.

I looked at my fob watch and touched my fingertips to the opposite wrist, but at seventy beats per minute, it was slower than mine. Was it Dr Wagstaff's?

"Who's there? Hello?" A woman's voice came from the bell.

Dr Wagstaff pointed at me and raised his eyebrows. I shook my head.

"Where am I? It's all over green, I can't see a thing," the voice said.

"Your voice is in Oxford. But where are you?" Dr Wagstaff said.

"Dover."

"Dover!" Dr Wagstaff's voice rose in pitch, and he ran his hands through his hair till it stood up in spikes. "A distance of one hundred and fifty miles!"

"My voice is in Oxford ... right-oh, I'm dreaming. I sat down for a tea break, must have nodded off. Well, san fairy ann."

"If you are happy to converse with us, please tell us who you are," I said. "I am Miss Euphemia Thorniwork—"

"—and I am Dr Quincy Wagstaff. We are mathematicians, working on wireless communication."

"Let's have a chin-wag, why not?" the voice said. "Something to do. Any minute now, Bert'll be shaking me, telling me to wake up toot sweet, time to get the bus out. I'm Tilly. I'm a clippie. But they needn't think it's going to be like it was. I'm not going back to skivvying at home. Nar-poo, they can't make me. I'm 21 now."

"Clippie?" I asked. "What is that?"

"Blimey, show your ignorance. I'm a bus conductress."

"A singular job, for a lady," I said.

"Lady? No time for that now," Tilly said. "There are thousands like me, working just as well as the men. Wish they paid us the same. They told us women to keep the home fires burning, but there was a lot more to do, and we did it. And I'm going to make sure we can keep on at it, and more."

"They intended you to shovel coal onto the fireplace? Would you not do that anyway?" I said.

"It's a figure of speech. Where've you been, on the moon? You must have heard them. You must have seen all those posters saying 'Women of Britain say Go'. I don't know, this serves me right for eating a cheddar sandwich for my tea, always gives me dreams. Lucky to get any cheese, with the rationing."

Dr Wagstaff leaned toward the machine, eyes wide, rubbing his hands together. "What rationing? Who is restricting your diet?"

"The butcher and the baker and the grocer! Where do you do your shopping? There might not be rationing in cushy Oxford, but we've got it. It's alright for some. We might've won the war, but you wouldn't think so to look at the food."

"To what war do you refer?" I said.

Tilly snorted. "What are you, a pair of conchies? Only the Great

War, of course. The Kaiser's War. Only the war to end all wars."

My own heart seemed to freeze, then pound. My skin tingled. "Tilly." I heard my voice quaver. "What is today's date?"

"November the twenty second."

"Correct. And the year?"

"Blimey, you been asleep too? It's 1918." She coughed.

I grasped Dr Wagstaff's arm. "One hundred and fifty miles away, yes. And twenty-eight years."

"I don't like this place," Tilly said. "This green smoke is choking me. I'm trying to run but my legs won't move. Don't like those dreams. Wake up!"

Dr Wagstaff looked at one of the dials. "This is remarkable. It is not only her voice in the rolandic tube, it is her, it is her very essence. She is not in Dover, she is here. She is not yet born, today." He set his mouth into a line. "Tell us more about the war to end all wars."

"But why, when it is finished?" I said. "There is much more we could ask her."

Tilly coughed again. "Right, if you're so good at numbers, here are some. I heard that nearly 9 million soldiers copped it and nearly 30 million were injured. Like my brother Alfie. Went off to fight Fritz. Brought back as a cripple."

"I am sorry," Dr Wagstaff said. "But where was the war?"

"If I tell you, will I wake up?" Tilly spoke with a catch in her voice. "It was everywhere. Wars used to happen in faraway countries. But we could hear the guns firing in France, across the Channel."

I felt a wave of sorrow wash over me, for making her relive her terror. "It must have been horrifying," I said. I wished I could hold her hand, ask her about something else. Anything.

"Alfie told me. The mud. The thick slime in the trenches. Fat rats, gorged on flesh. Alfie said if you had a corpse to sit or stand on, you were lucky. And I saw it. I went to see a picture show about the Somme."

"What was that?" Dr Wagstaff asked. I could have struck him.

"A long battle. Two years ago. I saw what our boys had to go through. The trenches. Falling on the barbed wire. The pictures taken after the fighting were worse. Men lying helpless. The wounded being carried away. The pain in their faces."

"We cannot let this happen. How did the war start?" Dr

Wagstaff asked.

"I'm falling asleep," Tilly said. "But I'm dreaming. I'll wake up ... with a sick headache." Her heartbeat slowed. Fifty beats per minute. "Wake up. The tooter the sweeter."

"We must release her," I said. "Then she will find herself back, I mean forward, in her time."

Dr Wagstaff raised his hand. "How did it start, Tilly?"

Her voice shrank to a whisper. "Archduke got shot. Sarajevo. 1914. So tired."

"Archduke who? When?" Dr Wagstaff shouted at the cylinder, turning a knurled knob on the machine marked "volume control."

"The shot that echoed round the world. Sleep ... now." Forty-five beats per minute.

I grabbed his hand and pulled it away from the machine. "Let her go, Dr Wagstaff. She is losing consciousness. Her heartbeat is slowing. If you let her go, she may not survive, but if you hold her here, she will die. She cannot exist in two places at once. If she dies here, in her time not only does she not exist but she never has done. And never will."

"But if we can find out more, we can stop this abomination."

"How? Will you write to the Archduke and tell him not to go to Sarajevo in twenty-four years' time? We cannot kill Tilly. Let her go or she will die here and never be born. And nobody will know her, or her descendants. Think of what will never be. What might have been discovered." And the women who may never be helped to advance.

Forty beats per minute.

"If I let her go, I will find someone else to tell us more. To save all those lives." He reached a hand out toward the machine.

"No. It will kill whoever stays in it for more than a few minutes. Perhaps Tilly will not make a mark on history. Perhaps others would not either. But do they not also have the right to live? The end does not justify the means."

Dr Wagstaff's hand shook, then dropped to his side. He hung his head. "You put me to shame, Euphemia. I do not know if releasing her will send her to her own time." He brushed the back of his hand across his cheek, wiping away a tear. "But we must try reversing the polarity and boosting the current. Get another dry cell."

I ran to the shelf and brought back the remaining two. "Here—use all the power available."

With shaking hands, we connected them to the machine.

"Switch on the first cell!" Dr Wagstaff shouted.

Tilly's heart rate, still forty beats per minute, could just be heard over the sound of the bubbles gathering in the machine.

"And the second!"

A boom made my ears ring. I jumped back as the shards of the rolandic cylinder flew across the room. Green vapour billowed out of the shattered cylinder. I held my breath and grasped Dr Wagstaff by the sleeve. We ran to the door.

~

Dr Wagstaff sat on a wooden chair in the scullery with his head in his hands. "The Rolando study is over," he said. "I would not want to recreate the cylinder. The war will come and we cannot stop it. I am seventy-five years of age, I will not see men marching away to die as cattle. But you will."

I knelt down on the stone floor next to him. "It will come. We cannot stop it." I took his hand. "But Tilly called it the war to end all wars. Let us pray that she will be right."

———

Euphemia Thorniwork finished her mathematics degree with 1st Class Honours. She then went on to become a teaching fellow and was responsible for the development of the Lifschitz-Thorniwork equation. Shortly after this, Dr Lifschitz disappeared. All that Euphemia will say on the subject is that she plans to join him, as soon as she discovers a way into his world.

———

Judith Field lives in London, UK. She is the daughter of writers, and learned how to agonise over fiction submissions at her mother's (and father's) knee. She's a pharmacist working in emergency medicine, a medical writer, editor, and indexer. She started writing in 2009. She mainly writes speculative fiction, a welcome antidote from the world she lives in. Her work has appeared in a variety of publications in the USA, UK, and Australia. When she's not working or writing, she studies English, knits, sings, and swims, not always at the same time. She blogs at *Luna Station Quarterly*.

"The Fissure of Rolando" originally appeared in *Theian Journal*, November 2015.

THE NEW OPEC

An essay by Ollie Garky,
brought to our attention by E. B. Fischadler

Mr. (or Ms.) President:

I have an important proposal for the leaders of the western nations. If they are wise enough to adopt my plan, the West can establish control over the world's economy and have the most powerful political leverage in the history of the world.

A LESSON FROM HISTORY

History is replete with examples of military, political, or economic powers arising due to accidents of geography. England, where no citizen lives more than 100 miles from the ocean, became the great sea power of the 18th and 19th centuries. The United States, with its vast prairies turned to farmland, was known in the 20th century as the world's breadbasket.

Beginning in the latter half of the 20th century, a group of nations around the Persian Gulf were able to parley the vast oil reserves under their soil into control of much of the world's energy. These nations formed a cartel known as OPEC, the Oil Producing and Exporting Countries. OPEC was able to hold the world's energy reserves hostage over several decades, its countries going from poor desert lands to the world's wealthiest.

In the early 1970s, OPEC greatly curtailed oil exports in an attempt to boost prices. By so doing, they created a crisis in the

United States, at that time a world superpower. The effect was to permanently alter the economy of the U.S. and to establish OPEC as a world economic power.

What if the U.S. and western countries had some commodity that OPEC couldn't do without? If such a commodity existed and the western powers could organize to control its distribution, they would re-establish their control of the world economy.

It is by dint of extensive research and insightful and imaginative planning that I have established a plan for the United States and other western powers to regain parity with OPEC. In fact, when successfully implemented, my plan will allow the West to regain their prominent place in the world order. Like OPEC, the West has an accidental geographic advantage over the rest of the world. Following my design, this advantage will give the western world an economic stranglehold comparable, even superior, to that currently held by OPEC.

SEE THE FOREST FOR THE TREES!

OPEC is able to maintain its stranglehold on the west due to 1) OPEC sitting on the largest oil reserves in the world and 2) the dependence of western economies on oil. Neither of these is likely to change anytime soon. OPEC's reserves are large enough to last well into the next century. And despite significant efforts to develop alternate energy sources, the West still obtains most of its energy from oil. But there is a substance that is of vital importance to every country in the world, whether eastern or western. In fact, the importance of this substance vastly overshadows that of oil. Without this substance, oil cannot be converted to energy. Of far greater import, though, is that without this substance, life on Earth cannot continue. I am talking about oxygen.

The world relies on a cycle in which oxygen is converted to carbon dioxide and carbon dioxide is converted back to oxygen. The relative amounts of each gas in the atmosphere is maintained in a precise balance. Upset this balance too much and life fails. If there is not enough carbon dioxide, plant life fails. If there is not enough Oxygen, most[1] animal life fails.

---

[1] I am deliberately ignoring anaerobic organisms. These include rabies and various other ugly diseases. After all, wouldn't we be better off if they all

Every country needs vast amounts of oxygen for its citizens to breathe, and to burn fossil fuels such as oil and coal. The OPEC countries consume at least their share of the world's oxygen, especially since their recent wealth has allowed their upper classes to acquire Porsches, Bentleys, and Gulfstreams, all of which consume vast quantities of oxygen as they guzzle gas. Situated on vast deserts, these countries convert little if any carbon dioxide back to oxygen.

Western countries also consume substantial amounts of oxygen, turning much of it into carbon dioxide. The difference between the West and the East is that western countries also produce vast amounts of oxygen. How? By photosynthesis. Plants take carbon dioxide from the air and emit oxygen as a waste product. A large portion of the world's renewable supply of oxygen is produced by forests. It has been determined that 31% of the Earth's landmass is covered by forests. The United States alone accounts for almost 19% of the Earth's forests, with virtually all the remaining forest in Canada, South America and Europe. The OPEC countries, by contrast, have essentially zero forest, hence contribute nothing to their own or the world's oxygen supply.

THE NEW OPEC

Under my leadership, the Western Nations will form a cartel, The Oxygen Producing and Exporting Countries (OPEC).[2] This cartel would control the world's oxygen supply and have that other OPEC in a literal stranglehold. Just imagine being able to say, "Sell us oil at $50 a barrel or don't breathe." Even if the old OPEC saw this coming, it would take several decades for them to terraform[3]

---

died?

[2] Hereafter I, and soon the entire world, shall refer to the Oil Producing and Exporting Countries as the old OPEC, and the Oxygen Producing and Exporting Countries as OPEC.

[3] They'd have to somehow irrigate all that desert and probably condition the soil. Where we really have them by the neck is they would have to plant vast forests. Of course, we control the market in trees, so can further impede their comeback from our domination.

their lands and establish forests of their own. Meanwhile, the western nations control the flow of oxygen to the old OPEC.

Millions of Americans buy Donald Trump's plan to build a fence along the border with Mexico to keep out illegal immigrants. By that light, my plan is not terribly ambitious. OPEC can build a fence around the old OPEC to keep oxygen from flowing their way. Initially, my analysis showed that this fence would have to reach the stratosphere, approximately 6 miles high, and completely surround the old OPEC. I estimate the length of this fence to be 4,000 miles.

I have recently revised this estimate after seeing a picture of New York City covered in smog. This occurs when there is insufficient wind to move all the vehicle exhaust out of the city and fresh air into the city to replace it. So the fence need only be as tall as the buildings in New York, say 50 stories on average, to smother the old OPEC in smog. This translates to a height of only 600 feet.

Alternatively, we could simply plant large numbers of engines around the OPEC countries, with their air inlets pointed away from the old OPEC countries and their exhausts pointed toward the old OPEC. These engines would intercept the oxygen flowing into the region and convert it into carbon dioxide and other undesirable stuff, which would flow into the old OPEC.

If they are nice to us, we might open a gate in the wall, or shut down a subset of those engines. If not, we close the gates or floor the throttle on those engines and watch them gag.

THE ULTIMATE THREAT

It may be that the old OPEC will attempt to undermine this strategy by cutting off all oil exports. In such a dire crisis, OPEC could simply threaten to torch its forests. This would serve to generate vast amounts of carbon monoxide, carbon dioxide and other nasty combustion products, as well as eliminating the source of any future supply of oxygen. Soon, the entire world would be gasping for what little oxygen remains in the atmosphere. Of course that includes members of the new OPEC as well as members of the old OPEC. Hopefully, the old OPEC won't notice this little detail and our bluff would work. Under such a threat, the old OPEC would have to cave immediately.

WORLD DOMINATION

This is not a diatribe; I'm not obsessed with the old OPEC. I hold no personal grudge against the citizens of the Middle East. The West's control of the world's oxygen supply gives it leverage over any group, any country. Even the most irrational group of radicals, even the most deranged of dictators, knows they have to breathe. Through control of the world's oxygen, I offer the Western nations the ability to impose truth, justice and the American way over any group or nation.

OXYGEN PRODUCTION AND EXPLOITATION COMMISSION

I have gathered a group of subject matter experts into an organization prepared to serve the US government in creating OPEC. These experts include a worldwide network[4] of chemists who can measure the current levels of oxygen, the Office for Prediction of Exploitability Conditions. Oxygen management is achieved by three groups. The Office of Prescribed Exposure Control is prepared to deploy engines or a wall around a target area on a moment's notice. The Oxygen Production Engineering Council comprises retired woodsmen, who can titrate the number of trees in U.S. and European forests in order to regulate the amount of oxygen in the atmosphere to precise levels. In dire circumstances, the Office of Pyromania for Extreme Circumstances can implement the Ultimate Threat. Finally, the Office for Persuasion, Exhortation, and Consequences would realize the enormous leverage available by making threats.

These resources can all be made available to the U.S. government simply by appointing me to a senior cabinet level post: Oxygen Production and Exportation Commissioner, reporting directly to the President. Because of the extraordinary power I wield, I expect to be superior to the Joint Chiefs and all other cabinet officers. Of course, the post would come with the usual six figure salary and perks such as a wood paneled office and personal

---

[4] Currently the network extends from Secaucus to Parsippany, New Jersey. When I am appointed to my cabinet post, I shall immediately extend its reach to the rest of the world.

Gulfstream V.

I eagerly await your response to my Offer to Provide Economic Control.

O. Garky

Member, Organization of Practicing Engineer Crackpots

Ollie Garky leads a small group of people dedicated to exploiting the West's control of oxygen in order to restore the western countries power over the rest of the world. These same people are also dedicated to gaining control of the Western countries, or producing economic chaos.

E. B. Fischadler has been writing short stories for several years, and has recently begun publishing. His stories have appeared in *Mad Scientist Journal, Bewildering Stories, eFiction, Voluted Tales, Beyond Imagination Literary Magazine*, and *Beyond Science Fiction*. In addition to fiction, Fischadler has published over 30 papers in refereed scientific journals, as well as a chapter of a textbook on satellite engineering. When he is not writing, he pursues a career in engineering and serves his community as an EMT. Fischadler continues to write short stories and is working on a novel about a naval surgeon. You can learn more about Fischadler and access his other publications at: https://ebfischadler.wordpress.com/

CALVANTE'S MAIDEN

An essay by Dr. Henrietta Bolingbroke,
as provided by Bobby O'Rourke

[Excerpt from "The Madness of Giacomo Calvante" by Dr.
Henrietta Bolingbroke, originally published in *New Italian Literary
Studies*, 22 June 2015]

... intensely excited to be among the first to peruse the newly
discovered diaries of poet Giacomo Calvante. These diaries may
shed light not only on his poetry—the influence of which has long
been underestimated—but also on a theorized mental illness and
even madness which may have caused his premature death.

Calvante was born in Turin, Italy, in 1781, an obscure pioneer
of free verse and a sympathizer with the Romantic movement
prevalent in England at the time. Calvante's poetry, like that of the
Romantics, emphasized a break from traditional verse and an
intense focus on the passions as the guiding force for humanity.
Despite these sensibilities, Calvante was an outspoken proponent
of technological innovation and a gifted student of chemistry and
engineering; he did not revile the Industrial Revolution as many
Romantics did. Consider the following lines from Calvante's
unpublished poem "Some Words on Coleridge":

We strive
though our bodies turn to dust.
Even so
there exists a spark that lights the future.
If we must admire any part of man,

admire the will to mold a cup of iron,
which can house life forever.
An eternal mind deserves an eternal frame.

Calvante maintained a consistent output of poetry, but very few of his poems were published in his lifetime. Only two books, *The Automaton* (1808) and *As I Look Forward* (1814) were published by friends, and the first of these saw little circulation. Calvante kept hundreds of poems in his desk, either never intending for them to be seen or never considering them ready for publication. It is also known that Calvante fell into "a pervasive melancholy" shortly after his second book was published, and he spent the remaining years of his life as a recluse. He was believed to have succumbed to tubercular breathing complications: his father owned and operated a Tuscan mineral mine, which Calvante visited regularly as an adolescent.

The Collected Works of Giacomo Calvante, compiled and released in 1925, was largely ignored, scholars dismissing the poet's influence on ...

~

[From Giacomo Calvante's diary, dated 7 December 1807]

My hand shakes as I write. I only stop now to scribble these words so if I may doubt myself in the future, I have proof of what I have done and what I have felt. Outside of these two acts, is there anything else?

My automaton is complete. She is alive. Even I, who know every crevice, and every imperfection of her, am in awe of the softness of her skin, the olivine shade of her eyes, the symmetry of her shoulders and bosom.

She is beautiful in the way gravity is constant, the way stars adhere to their natural course. She is beautiful because she will not age, will not degrade. She is beautiful because she is perfection.

Building her component parts was a long but ultimately fruitful task: my love of chemistry and construction as a small boy played no little part in her completion. Father used to allow me to peruse his bound copy of Vesalius's *On the Fabric of the Human Body*, and I recall spending entire days poring over the diagrams of the human frame. Mother thought it grotesque, but then again Father claimed her books of poetry led the mind into idle wanderings. I loved when Mother would read to me each night from her selection of poetry. I knew even then that language, in a way as mechanical and efficient as any machine, was also a conduit to something deeply immersed within us, a flame that undulates with the passions and is in fact "the fire within our furnace."

Having this dichotomy in mind, I thought of the best, most perfect way to introduce my automaton to the world. I read her poetry. And because of poetry she has awakened.

Materialists may say that she is powered by heat, which is merely a half-truth. I have made her from fire.

~

[From "The Madness of Giacomo Calvante"]

Although the dates and authenticity of the diaries have been verified, these bizarre writings beg the question: when did Calvante's delusion of a "metal maiden" begin?

After working alongside his father at the mine in Tuscany, Calvante traveled to Milan in 1800, where he began writing his poems in earnest and fraternizing with artists and philosophers sympathetic to his aesthetics. Strangely, none of these associates make mention in any of their correspondence of Calvante's delusions. Indeed, they seem to have been completely ignorant of it ...

~

[Calvante's Diary, 8 March 1808]

I have named her Regina. A queenly name for the woman who holds the future in her frame. She responds to this. Is a name all that is needed for an identity?

Regina cannot seem to grasp the origin of her existence, and Heaven knows I have tried to explain! She learns quickly and is quite adept at speech and writing, yet I cannot convey to her that I am her creator: in her mechanical mind, I am her benevolent friend and protector, but she has no inkling, or indeed impetus to learn, of her own origins.

I note that her memory seems to fade for varying periods of time. We have, for example, gone over the letter "R" many times in her alphabetical studies, and for many weeks she was unable to recall lessons we had reviewed only minutes before. This complication requires further study.

Aside from these difficulties, she is most astute and precocious. She has endless curiosity, and I have begun to teach her the rudiments of my craft. Regina delights in the throes of language, and has developed a particular fondness for Shakespeare. Is this not proof she is human in all but name?

~

[From the personal journal of Henrietta Bolingbroke, dated 16 March 2015]

Can't believe I got to handle the actual pages of Calvante's diaries today. Terrified to make even the slightest mark or tear.

So many friends have chided me for spending time on his poetry. He's a footnote, they say. Stick with the real Romantics, and the rest can jog on to the satanic mills. They might be right, but I always thought there was something special about him and his poetry. Here's proof. Even if that something special stems from insanity.

Strange dream I had last night: I am reading C.'s diaries and I fall into the pages. C. is there, yelling at me to add more coal to the fire. Thinking of line: "I have made her from fire." It's lovely, and a little scary.

~

[From "The Madness of Giacomo Calvante"]

Calvante's first book of poems, *The Automaton* was published in late 1808. Its dedication to "The Woman of the Future" has most often been thought to be in honor of Lisl von Welthaus, a German émigré from Bavaria. It is apparent at one time Calvante and Welthaus were lovers, though how long their relationship lasted has never been verified.

~

[Calvante's Diary, 26 January 1809]

Never in all my days has such a river of inspiration flown through me! And all in the name of Regina!

For the first time in my life, I have had the courage to ask dear Theodoro to publish my work. He of course has been asking for many years to publish my work, such a kind friend. With Regina by my side, a perfect vessel by which to test my poetry, I have unbridled confidence. I have read to her all of my poems, determining the strength of each poem by her reaction to their pathos. I trust her to recognize such language that touches the very heart and sets it alight.

Lisl is upset I have been shut up all this time with my work (and Regina, though I have told not a soul of my darling's existence). Lisl will come to understand in time that I have been preoccupied with escorting poetry itself towards a new dawn, one where the passions and the intellect of man have united in the cause of a universal experience.

~

[From "The Madness of Giacomo Calvante"]

After the lackluster reception of the literary community to *The Automaton*, associates of Calvante began to notice the poet's withdrawal from life. Friends blamed the stress of the book's perfunctory debut, but these diaries indicate his growing paranoia about the "automaton" may have been the cause of this social reclusion. Intuitions that one is being persecuted, or that one is not in control of one's actions, are common amongst those suffering from mental illnesses ...

~

[Calvante's Diary, 4 April, 1812]

I shall never know carnal longing or the scent of wine,
I will forget I am glass on which a hand rests—
It must be sad to be a mirror, a surface waiting to be whole.
If I am not mine, I am not the prisoner of Time.

A scrap of parchment with these words upon it was on my writing desk as I awoke this morning. She wrote it. Regina wrote this for me. My creation has a mind of her own.

Why then can I not stop weeping?

I have spent my whole life composing lines upon lines of drivel, just to have a taste of what true artistic genius feels like. I have been trodden underfoot by giants, by Shelley's and Byron's words and the whole rotting lot. I love them, and I hate them for being what I can never be, even if I lived to write for two hundred years.

My automaton—this, this thing—has surpassed me. I know because when I reached the last word, I felt within me a sadness that reaches beyond tears and makes contact with the inner soul. I never wanted to leave the poem, no matter how bleak and despairing it may have been. Once I finished reading that small scrap of parchment, I turned and saw her standing behind me, her face beaming in anticipation and joy.

"Look what I have done," she said, her voice, which I had once associated with the soft wind blowing over the sea, like the diving screech of a hawk. In her outstretched hands, she held more parchment filled with dozens of poems.

How warm the fireplace seemed to me at that moment. How it would welcome those delicious pieces of parchment.

... Now that it is night and I have ordered Regina to retire, my head has cooled enough to write again.

How does she render life so beautifully? I think it is because poets seek to confront emptiness. All we long for is an answer to why we are here, and the fact we will never find this answer is the source of poetry's attraction. We view ourselves from above and realize how small we are in the vast cosmos. How noble then is our pursuit of love and friendship when all things are destined to crumble and turn to dust! Not so Regina. She will never crumble, never decay. Her isolation is complete, as she will never know another creature that can tread the sands of time unscathed.

Because she is perfect, she is alone. So her words reflect that loneliness in a way we can only begin to fathom.

I have heard it said that geniuses are lonely because they live as if in another world; few others can reach the peaks on which they stand. Today I feel as though I have discovered my own peak is only a hill in the shadow of a mountain.

~

[Bolingbroke's Journal, 11 April, 2015]

Work on the Calvante diaries and the article exhausting. Not sleeping very well. Finding the diaries more disturbing as I go along. The line "it must be sad to be a mirror" especially. Whenever I hear someone saying they feel like they're being used, or that they can't express their own feelings at the expense of others, I say "don't go through life as a mirror." I think I picked it up from my father, but I can't remember.

Whoever said this was right: never meet your heroes. Calvante is turning out to be something I don't like, a jealous lout and misogynist. But that's the illness, I'm sure. Can't blame him for that.

~

[From "The Madness of Giacomo Calvante"]

As I Look Forward, published in 1814, was much more successful than *The Automaton*, and it brought Calvante to the attention of such poets as Shelley and Keats. Calvante, however, immediately scorned the success of the book and would hardly speak of it when asked about his success or forthcoming writing. His publisher and friend Theodoro DiFabio pleaded with Calvante to continue his work and publish a new book. Calvante refused, and his paranoiac tendencies intensified. He hardly left his home and cut his friends and correspondence from his life. No one close to the poet was able to find out the cause of his distress, but these diaries suggest that ...

~

[Calvante's Diary, 11 February, 1816]

My chest aches, and not only from my wracking cough. My heart feels composed of lead, and I believe it is trying to sink into darkness. I should let it. All the poems in *As I Look Forward* belong to Regina, not me. Writing this does not bring me the relief of confession, but it does soothe my self-hatred. Every day she places a poem on my desk with her delicate right hand, the hand which bears the sickle moon scar—one of countless sophomoric mistakes I made during her construction. Every day I read, unable to stop myself from gorging on her tragic, elegant language. Every poem takes something from me, then gives it back tenfold. I recognize my own smallness and isolation, but I am forced to connect with another isolated voice in the darkness. She expands my soul. I cannot escape the lines of her poem "On Richard II":

We are all of us this miscast king
Grasping at what we say is mine, I, my,
When in truth our lives are marbled mistakes
Brought by Accident's arms into eternity.

I hate her. I hate her.

She loses memory of writing these poems, a side-effect of her creation I can never explain. It happened one day in 1814, when spring had reared its all-too-happy head, that I, drunk beyond reckoning, collected as many of her poems as I could find, and sent them off to Theodoro. He is an unwitting accomplice to plagiarism. Maybe he will find solace in Lisl's bed, where I know he has been spending most of his nights of late.

I have called myself a poet for so long, I do not know how to be anything else. Am I some kind of half-crazed Jupiter, creating life and shunning it when it upsets me? Am I mad?

I long to exist in darkness for a while, where I can hear no scratch of the quill, see no smile of the girl who believes she pleases me when she shows me her work.

~

[Bolingbroke's Journal, 21 May, 2015]

Don't feel well. Went to doctor, said everything is fine. Suggested a shrink if memory lapses become worse. I forget where I am sometimes, other times I can't remember who my parents were, how long I've lived in my flat. Sometimes I think I remember things that never happened to me.

~~Herb Harry Dad's name is Harold Harrison~~
~~My goddamned father's name is~~
shit shit I can't remember

I have a scar on my right hand. Bicycle accident when I was eight. Shape of sickle moon

~

[From "The Madness of Giacomo Calvante"]

... So where does this "metal maiden" find her place in the literary canon?

Of course, she was not real. Calvante's automaton was obviously a metaphorical muse, a conjured specter by which he could focus and dedicate his work. In the first few years of his published life, this muse served him well. It was only when success loomed large in the view of Calvante that he panicked. Unable to handle the sudden celebrity and notoriety of a famous poet, Calvante's health and spirit broke down, and his muse morphed into a demon who haunted his every step. The poems Calvante stashed in his desk from 1815–1822 are equally as beautiful as those in *As I Look Forward*, but he was most likely too frightened to let them see the light of day. Calvante's end is a sad one, succumbing not only to madness but also to a lung disease alone in his Milan rooms. His burial was paid for with the money he earned from his second book.

~

[Bolingbroke's Journal, 12 June, 2015]

Regina → Latin for "Queen"
Queen → female monarch, equivalent to male "king"
Henry Bolingbroke → Henry IV, king of England, usurper of Richard II
Henrietta → female form of Henry
Henrietta Bolingbroke → female king Henry

oh god I remember

~

[Calvante's final entry, 18 July, 1822]

I can only write this in between the fits of coughing. No one will read this, so I am not concerned with the blood splatters on the pages.

It seems fitting I should die with only Regina by my side. She has killed me, after all: I believe the pollution from her frame has infiltrated my lungs, and I can hardly breathe. I have ordered her to burn these writings when I die, but who knows if her memory will fail her again? She seems unable to grasp the concept of death. I wonder how she will confront this utterly foreign enemy.

All that will survive of me is this automaton and the words I have passed off as my own. I thought of seeking absolution from her, telling her I am a thief of her genius. But could she understand? Would she care? She is, after all, my creation, so am I not therefore within my rights to claim her work as my own?

Even as I write those words, I feel what little good is left inside escape from me like water from a broken canteen.

... I have just told her I love her and sent her away. I have neither the strength nor desire to destroy her. I have sent a true orphan into the world. All I can give her now is my blessing. And what little love still exists inside me.

Word has just reached me that Percy Shelley has died by drowning. I would not put it past the proud miscreant to have killed himself in order to maintain a posthumous reputation. His poetry is fine, but I much more enjoyed his wife's delightful tale on the resurrection of corpses.

~

[Bolingbroke's final entry, 23 June, 2015]

For how long have I been Henrietta Bolingbroke? Who else have I been?

I feel like I have lived my whole life in front of a shuttered window, believing there was an ocean behind it because I could hear the waves and the seagulls and smell the salt in the air. Only when I removed the shutter did I realize I had constructed all those sensations in my mind, and I look out on an unending stretch of desert sand.

I am not me. I owe my existence to that madman, that deviant. He made me his daughter-bride. Nothing I have or have done is mine. Even my words are his.

Who would do this? Who could be so lonely?

... It has occurred to me that in time I will forget what I have discovered about Calvante and his metal maiden. Only so many years or decades until I forget what I am and become something else. I may be alone, but I have the greatest gift of all: I will forget I am alone. Calvante never had that. He did at least one thing right, and that was an accident.

A romantic notion: I can walk the earth forever, writing the poetry I love and scattering it along the ground like apple seeds in the spring. I will confront eternity and make it bearable for those who cannot stand to look so far forward. I will hold someone's hand as they die.

Although I cannot remember, I have done it before.

▬▬▬▬▬▬▬▬▬▬▬▬▬

Henrietta Bolingbroke is a graduate student at St. Didian's University, closing in on her PhD in Comparative Literature with a concentration in Romantic Poetry. She is the recipient of the 2014 Madeline Chollet Memorial Poetry Prize, and her poetry has appeared in *Conroy's*, *Lost Ramblings Quarterly*, and the *Underground Review*. Henrietta's dissertation, "The Madness of Giacomo Calvante," will complete her course of study.

Bobby O'Rourke is a native of New Jersey. He has had fiction appear in *The Binnacle*, *Sanitarium Magazine*, and *The Writing Disorder*, and has had poetry appear in *Spires*. He recently earned his MA from Fairleigh Dickinson University in Creative Writing and Literature. While formerly a teacher, he now works in higher education administration. When Bobby is not writing, he reads, sings in his car or at karaoke, and enjoys popping in a truly horrendous horror movie for laughs. Bobby is currently throwing his first novel around to any agent kind enough to take a peek.

FURTHER INVESTIGATIONS ON A NEW SPECIES OF GIANT CARNIVOROUS OSTRACOD

A letter by Professor Tiberius Earwig Ph.D., FGS,
as provided by Dr Rebecca Siân Pyne

Dear Sir/Madam,

I admit that when I heard my research assistant screaming in mortal agony that overcast Tuesday morning in June, I naturally just assumed that he had been his usual careless self. For some reason, I cannot seem to attract the same caliber of minions that I did even a decade ago, but James was the most incompetent of them all. On reflection, he should have been vaporized with extreme prejudice after burning down my laboratory for the second time in as many months and blaming it on Igor.

Igor just happened to be on a two-week walking tour of Transylvanian graveyards and other sites of interest, but the idiot boy tried to pin it on him anyway.

You just can't get the staff these days.

When I opened the door into the aquarium room, the screaming had mercifully stopped. It was probably just as well I spent all that money on adequate sound proofing, or the neighbors would have complained. Splashes of fresh blood alerted me to the fact that a different and more terminal calamity had befallen my unlucky subordinate. My new specimen was out of her tank and gorging on his flesh. Gore turned the elegantly ornamented carapace crimson as razor sharp claws gouged it to bite sized pieces. Once I ascertained that his dying struggles had not damaged the subject, I was able to appreciate perfection and study the feeding behavior.

Never waste a scientific opportunity, as my mentor Dr. Frankenstein III always used to say before his unfortunate accident (if you can call a dozen angry villagers with pitchforks and flaming torches an accident).

She proved to be a highly adaptable predator, able to hunt on land as well as in the water, beautiful in its design. Based on my experience with related genera, I was able to identify her as female based on the inflated shape of the carapace, males usually being more elongated. Specimen 16-001-TEC/3 (Miranda as I call her in more intimate moments) came from the deepest part of the Irish Sea, a lucky find when I descended into the depths in a submersible rover craft and found a thriving colony.

Igor never said that he was claustrophobic and waited until we reached the bottom to tell me. If the submarine ejector seat I had been working on for years had actually worked, he would have been out of the hatch in an instant and left to swim home. As it was, there was a small fire and black smoke that hung around with nowhere to go until he fetched the extinguisher.

The look on his lop-sided face, the kind of face that not even a mother can love, was one of utter disdain—but it might just have been trapped wind. When someone looks like he does, it is difficult to be certain.

The scientific world knows Class Ostracoda only as small crustaceans that live in a calcareous, bivalved shell, more like a cockle than a crab. This was something entirely new, and it revitalized my career, which had waned ever since the Geological Society unfairly suspended me for conduct unbecoming one of its fellows. All I did was evaporate a keynote speaker at their last conference when her talk bored me to extreme violence. Is that really such a crime? Which of us has not thought about doing the same thing? The only difference is that I had a blaster ray and took action.

My discovery was my ticket back into the academic fold, the greatest biological find of the century. For one thing, of more than seventy thousand known species (of which only thirteen thousand are extant), most are only 1mm in length, with a few giants extending to 30mm.

My colleagues were all astounded when I formally described

Vampyrocythereis infernalis (Earwig, Pyne, Jones & Radchenko, 2016) in the *Proceedings of Deep Sea Biology*.

Many openly accused me of fraud. Others implied it. There was no such thing as a two-meter-long flesh eating Podocopid, they all said in a barrage of letters that kept the journal editors busy for weeks. It doesn't exist, they all said, willfully ignoring the press conference that proved on national television that it did.

Poor James got careless, a casualty of science. I take no responsibility for his death and feel no guilt.

Why on earth should it make me feel guilty?

He was warned not to get too close to the tank whenever16-001-TEC/3 was hungry and knew she had a preference for live prey.

When I stepped over a pile of stripped bone, my beautiful creature stopped her meal and raised feathered antennae as if in greeting. She had grown since I brought her up from the depths, thriving on a steady diet of paper boys, Jehovah's Witnesses, and the occasional unfortunate research assistant. I would not have to feed her again for some time. Over millennia, deep sea creatures have adapted to the low nutrient conditions in the abyss, so their metabolisms are slow. One rather scrawny post-graduate student would last at least a month.

By that time, another assistant will be in the post. I can only hope he or she lasts longer than the last one. Miranda did not seem inclined to attack me as I turned the CD player on and pressed play. She returned to the aquarium to begin the long drawn out business of digestion.

From a detailed literature review, no researcher has ever analyzed a two-and-a-half-meter-long carnivorous ostracod's appreciation for Mozart, and it will be the subject of a forthcoming paper in the *Journal of Applied Marine Biology and Musicology* (Earwig, 2017, in press).

Let the naysayers all call me a charlatan and question my sanity, but I put it to you that I am as sane as any other professional mad scientist in a world that thrives on sensationalist headlines.

Yours in Science,
Professor Tiberius Earwig

Professor Tiberius Earwig, BSc (Bristol), MSc (Aberystwyth), PhD (Cambridge), is an internationally recognized authority on fossil and recent Ostracoda, with two hundred papers in *The Journal of Micropalaeontology, Revista Española de Micropaleontología, Proceedings of the Ussher Society, Deep Sea Biology, Applied Biology and Musicology,* and others. After a brief sabbatical at Her Majesty's Asylum for Criminally Insane Academics, he retired to Whitby, but continues research. Professor Earwig is a member of Anti-Cites, an exclusive dining club which puts the world's rarest species on the menu. Other interests include Elizabethan Madrigal singing. He writes Shakespearean sonnets and evil haiku.

Dr Rebecca Siân Pyne is a writer, researcher (and mental health first-aider), now based in West Wales, via Cardiff University and the Swiss Federal Institute of Technology, Zurich. She has a PhD in Micropalaeontology, specializing in British Upper Cretaceous ostracods, with published research in *Revista Española de Micropaleontología* and *Palaeogeography, Palaeoclimatology, Palaeoecology.* Short stories have appeared in *Bête Noire, Macabre Cadaver, Bards and Sages Quarterly, Albedo One, Aurora Wolf, Eschatology, Neo-Opsis,* and others. Research assistants include a mad sprollie (springer spaniel x collie) who ensures there is no time for writer's block.

THE FATALISM OF THE AUTOMATONS
An account by Captain Walter Budanov and Samuel Walter, as provided by Jon Hartless

───────────────

Captain Budanov's diary, whaling vessel Demeter.

October 4th, 1886

Three months now in these ice floes. Petersburg seems but a distant memory, one I despised when there with its drinking and dancing and shallow fun. But now, as I look at great chunks of irregular ice, some as tall as mountains, hemming us in on all sides, I remember only the good times in the city. The warmth. The food. The companionship of men and women on dry land. But these mountains of ice will not allow us to return. If they so choose, they will crush us and send us to our graves. It is all in their implacable will!

~

October 14th

Finally, the ice has cracked! Rivulets are forming, sweeping us along to our ultimate fate—either the open sea and safety, or farther into the ice where the ship, and our hopes, will be crushed. For although we are Russian and resigned to our fate, we still blaspheme by secretly hoping to live. Still, whatever is done is done. We are powerless against destiny. I take great solace from this. The fate of the crew is not on my hands.

~

November 3rd

Astonishment rules today! Even First Mate Zbignew, a stoic who never wept a tear when told of the death of his wife, was amazed enough to shout in disbelief as his incredulous eyes fell upon the impossible this noon time. A boat! A small lifeboat, pushed by the sluggish water, kept on a course toward our vessel by the icebergs that form a narrow corridor.

More astonishment! The boat, when hooked by Ivan and Timor, was full of provisions! Carefully stored vodka, salted pork, rifles and cartridges, hunting knives, blankets, clothes and bags of gold. So much gold! All neatly packed away, as though someone saw his doom approaching yet had time enough to stock the lifeboat before fleeing from his destiny. We shall spend the rest of the day sorting the loot. We may yet die, but we die rich!

~

November 4th

It has just gone midnight and controversy rages across the *Demeter*, warming the crew far more than the dispirited paraffin stove that splutters in the galley. Accursed fate had one more mocking trick to play upon us, one more scornful slap to deliver. There was a man on the lifeboat! Curled up in the very rear end, buried under piles of fur and clothes.

The doctor—curse him and his unintelligible French mutterings!—forced us to take the man into the doctor's own cabin. A wise choice. My crew would have happily thrown the man overboard to protect their share of the lifeboat's rich bounty. "After all," as First Mate Zbignew reasoned, "the stranger would have died without us, so it is no blood on our hands to speed up what Fate has already decided."

"But are you certain of that?" demanded Ivan of the crew.

"I am patient," replied Timor. "I will wait. The man will not survive long. Not on this ship. Fate will play its hand and we will yet be rich."

The argument ran long into the night. I left them to it. A wrong word out of place and not even my rank would protect me from a harpoon in my back ...

~

November 4th

The man lives. Another curse upon him, and a thousand more upon the interfering doctor and his decadent belief that every life matters! Worse, the man grows stronger. Our one hope is that his mind has been shattered by the exposure. A madman, after all, cannot do an inventory of his lifeboat. My hopes are high—or as high as I can ever permit them to be, which is not so very high, after all—but the man raves and screams about giant men, slaves of silver and gold, taking over the world. Agh, he must be mad! All will be well.

~

November 5th

All is not well. The man recovers. He speaks weakly, but rationally. My one hope? He has no answer for what he is doing so far from home, or how he came to be in the lifeboat at all. If he is an undocumented man, then the booty is ours! Tonight, he will tell me everything. I will take the interfering doctor with me to record all that he says. I will have the truth, even if it crushes me!

~

November 6th

I am crushed. I can write no more as I fearfully scan the horizon for the ship of soulless creatures I now know to be out there. Curse this ice! Curse this sea! If we get out of this, I swear I will never even sail across a small lake in the future!

~

I will not test your patience by withholding my identity any more. I am Samuel Walter of Newcastle. Ah! I see my fame has spread even out here! The international press, no doubt? How many column inches did my artistry receive? But my dear sir, it *was* art. Who else but an artist could have worked his canvas with such consummate skill? To peel back the skin, to delicately work around the sinew, to open the skull so neatly?

But I see you wince; strange that a man who spends his days butchering such beautiful creatures as whales should be so sensitive when it is man being slaughtered, but I will respect your sensibilities. See, I too have delicacy and tact. I also have sharp eyes. I see you looking in fear at the dinner knife on my plate, but do not worry; my art is satiated. It would gain no fulfilment in such uncongenial surroundings. In any case, the knife is far too blunt to be of any use to me.

Besides, I must tell you of the horror I have faced out here in the freezing sea. I made my hurried retreat from home some weeks ago after the police finally got wind of my artistic endeavours. I had already planned for the eventuality and I slipped away to the docks and stowed away on a vessel bound for Russia. My mother was Russian and I speak the language well, don't you agree?

The Pride of Japan—and I have no idea where that name came from, someone was being whimsical somewhere—was nothing more than a schooner with about a dozen passengers and crew. On the way out of the Liverpool docks, I could already feel my artistic tendencies rising within me. Try as I might, I could not contain them. After all, I had never worked on board a ship before, and I found the challenge to be most rewarding.

Alas, I allowed my artistic freedom too much reign. Soon, I was alone on the vessel, and being a gentleman, I had no idea how to sail a ship, how to change course, nothing. Oh, how I bitterly repented my exuberant but natural folly as the vessel was swept along by tides and eddies to who knows where? Fortunately, I had a liberal supply of meat, a great deal of drinking water in the hold, and a resilient attitude to stand foursquare and take whatever life threw at me.

Of course, I had no idea what life was about to throw at me ...

It must have been on the 25th day after we left Liverpool that I saw the ship. At first, it was a strange, bright twinkle on the horizon, and I dismissed it as being nothing more than a low star in the night sky. I was still dismissing it thirty minutes later and an hour after that, but when I came up on deck the next morning and saw the twinkle was still there, and still in the same relative position to my uncontrolled vessel, I realized it was something artificial, and I rushed to the captain's cabin to borrow his telescope.

Can you imagine my delight on seeing the blurred outline of another vessel? I knew fate would hand me something if I stayed firm and resolute. Ahead of me was my salvation. Or so I thought. I sent a distress flare upward and dashed to retrieve my belongings—my knives, my diary, some clothing, and a small amount of gold and silver, all supplemented by jewellery from the crew and passengers who, after all, would no longer require such earthly gewgaws.

As I feverishly bound my bundle together, ensuring that the tools of my trade were safely wrapped and hidden under several layers of impedimenta, I began to wonder what had been flashing on the horizon. Had I realized what was waiting for me, I would have stayed below decks and refused to come out, but venture out I did.

Great God, the sight I saw! Even now I can barely recall it without astonishment. Bursting back onto the deck I was almost blinded by an unnatural glare. Ripples of silver and gold washed over the bare wooden beams of *The Pride of Japan*, while rainbow lights exploded and reformed all around me. I flung my hands across my eyes with a cry of pain, yet still the bright light burned through the gaps between my fingers.

Gradually, however, my eyes grew stronger, and I risked peering across the deck. The intense light was evaporating all the shadows habitually thrown by the schooner's mast and cabins. I peered round in every direction, but it was only when I staggered a few steps to one side that the blinding, shimmering light finally resolved itself into an identifiable body.

I gaped in stupefaction. A vessel, several hundred feet long, was next to the schooner. Although it was shaped like a traditional ship, there the similarities ended, for this craft was constructed of some form of highly polished alloy—that which was not gold was silver, and that which was not silver seemed to be diamond. The ship lacked both masts and funnels, leaving its source of power unidentified.

This, however, was nothing to my amazement at what was revealed next. I gazed up at the impossible hull, my eyes failing to make out any fine details against the brightly reflected light, when a movement up on top caught my notice. I squinted, trying to defuse the haze of light surrounding the ship. An outline appeared, and I saw in fear and astonishment that I was looking directly at a giant man of silver and gold!

I cannot begin to express my fear at this point. Was this a ship of demons come to take my immortal soul to everlasting torment, or a ship of angels come to save me? Surely, I thought to myself in terror, surely I deserved redemption, for no soul is out of reach of our Lord Jesus Christ if one prays hard enough? Accordingly, I fell to my knees and prayed to the silver man, exulting the greatness of God, hoping for mercy while keeping one eye on the fearful creature.

I vaguely supposed that my untarnished soul would be lifted from my sinful body and I would soar to the heavens. Instead, there was a grinding noise, a series of explosive hisses, and to my bewilderment, a huge door suddenly swung down from the side of the enormous silver vessel. The door was hinged at the bottom and thus it doubled as a ramp as the end touched the wooden deck of the schooner. I stared fearfully into the interior of the vessel but the bright shining light obscured any details within. I was aware of some sort of room or corridor behind the door, but nothing more.

Something stirred within the doorframe and I saw two more of the silver men appear and look down on me. I had thought the lone figure on the top deck to be special, unique, the undoubted leader of the souls on board, but I now realised that he was no different to the others. The entire crew must have been made up of these Herculean creatures. The two figures walked down the ramp, their movements strange to my eyes; they walked well, but without the fluid gait that characterizes the living. It was as though each movement existed individually from the next, and I was watching a tableaux of movement rather than a continuous whole.

The creatures walked past me and disappeared below decks. I peered after them, wondering if I should follow, wondering what they would make of my artistry that lay decomposing down below.

A faint hissing noise made me turn around, and I shrieked in surprise and terror; another of the silver men had somehow walked down the ramp without me hearing it and was now looking down at me, no more than a foot away.

It was formed like a Greek statue, with an impressive chest and limbs to match. I peered nervously at the rest of the creature and caught my breath; the joints were not smooth and organic—they consisted of some form of hinge and screws. They were not alive. They were automatons! Scarcely had I made this deduction, the creature grasped the back of my coat, lifted me bodily off the deck, and carried me up the silver walkway and into that mysterious, terrifying vessel.

I was swiftly conveyed along shining corridors of silver, until we reached what looked like a blank wall of the same reflective material. The automaton holding me raised its huge hand and pressed a small golden switch set in a swirl of ornately designed leaves. I gasped as the solid wall moved forward—it was another hatch, like the one I had seen outside, one that closed so perfectly against the surrounding wall that the seam was invisible.

I was taken inside and saw in astonishment that I was in a wood-panelled study. An electric lamp stood on a wooden desk, a well-stuffed leather chair was standing a small distance from the desk, and various brass scientific instruments lined the far wall. A door opened and a tall human figure strode through, stopping in surprise and displeasure when he beheld me and the automaton in his sanctum.

"What is the meaning of this?" he cried, his Russian accent harsh on my ears, so different to the lyrical, gentle flow of words made by my late mother's lips. "Why have you disturbed me? Who is this person?"

The automaton opened its mouth; I was conscious of the sound of some machinery winding up, rather like a clock. There was a gentle but definite thump, like a clock about to chime, and a soothing, articulate voice floated from the open mouth! "There was a distress flare, Captain Krylov. We answered it."

"What the hell is it to me if a ship is in distress?" thundered the captain. "I have turned my back on the world, and on humanity, yet you bring humanity to me! I won't have it, you hear? I won't!"

"We saw the distress flare; we answered it," repeated the automaton, smoothly.

"I gave you no such order," snarled the man, glaring at me in an unfriendly manner.

"Yet we answered it," said the automaton, its mouth still open.

"So, already it begins," hissed Krylov, fear and anger battling across his swarthy face. "First you defy me, then you will overthrow me."

The automaton closed its mouth. Again the winding noise was heard, followed by the soft thump, before the mechanical man opened its mouth again. "We must follow our programming, as you must follow yours. The crew are dead. Murdered."

"What, all of them?" exclaimed Krylov, his interest aroused despite himself.

"All but this man."

"How do you explain that?" The strange captain asked, glowering at me.

"It was the first mate," I replied, trying to remain calm against the waking nightmare I found myself in. "He must have been a mad man! He killed all the crew and passengers until only I was left, and then he came for me! I was fortunate; I was able to deal him a mortal blow as we struggled."

"Why should I believe you?" asked Krylov, staring at me in deep dislike.

"You may check the evidence of the ship," I replied, after pretending to think. "You will find the first mate's journal, detailing his bloodthirsty spree. I found it in his cabin after he attacked me."

"Well?" grunted the captain to the automaton, which opened its mouth and again wound up its voice box.

"He lies."

"It can pick up respiration, eye dilation, sweat secretion, and a dozen other signifiers which reveal your lies," the captain said with a grin as I gasped in shock, his eye looking at me speculatively. "So, you are a mass murderer and a liar, hey? A man standing against convention and morality? Maybe that makes you the only free man in the world ... A murderer cast as the only free individual? The vicious irony appeals to me! Humph! The world is a theatre of cruelty, and we are its helpless puppets! Walk with me, man, and listen as I explain what is going on here."

"Where are you going, Captain Krylov?" asked the mechanical man, its smooth face sliding round, watching its master.

"I cannot go anywhere that you cannot find me," snapped the

Russian, his tone bitter. "My fate is sealed. Rest assured of that, my mechanical marvel. Rest assured of that!"

He gestured at me and I followed him from the wooden study, back into the silver and gold vessel. We walked brightly lit corridors, though whether the light came from the reflective walls or hidden fittings I can say not.

"What do you think of my vessel, sir?" demanded the captain.

"It is astonishing," I blurted. "What is the power source? How does it move without sails? Wherever did you obtain it? And the crew!"

"The power source is my secret; suffice to say, it can push a vessel through the roughest seas far faster than any steam vessel. The navigation and control likewise are my secret; I did not spend my entire life, and sacrifice so much, to reveal them to anyone who asks!"

"And the crew?" I asked, timidly, for I was conscious of being completely in the madman's power.

"My own creations, may my hands be cut off for the foolishness in creating them! I knew! Even as I fashioned them in my secret workshops, I knew what my fate would be if I continued!"

"And what do you believe your fate shall be? What role will the crew have in it?"

"My inevitable doom," replied the captain, calmly, stalking along the vessel and refusing to answer any further questions on the topic. I instead asked him more about the ship, which he was clearly very proud of, in order to please his vanity and make him look favourably upon me.

"What do you call this splendid ship?" I asked after several fulsome minutes of praise.

"I call her *The Goddess of Mercy*, in the hope that any such Goddess will smile favourably upon me, should she exist, which I doubt, but I cannot be sure, hence my cautious pieties to the possibility of her existence. Ah, see here, this will interest a man such as yourself," exclaimed Krylov, operating a small switch which caused a hidden door to swing silently open.

I peered into the room; three of the towering mechanical men stood within, tending banks of machinery in which dials flickered and lights flashed on and off. I realised as I stepped forward that there were several projectiles at the front of the room, all attached to the banks of scientific instruments. As I walked down the side of them, I guessed their function from the shape.

"Cannons?" I asked, doubtfully, for they were all smooth tubes with no visible firing mechanism, or indeed any way of loading a cannon ball.

"High frequency emitters," corrected the captain. "Far superior to any conventional cannon. Open the blast doors," he commanded the mechanical men. The three figures straightened but did not immediately respond, causing Krylov to explode in Russian expletives. "Open the blast doors, damn you," he snarled when he had finished swearing. "I am still the captain of this vessel and you will obey me!"

The automatons finally turned and operated various controls. With a hiss of compressed air, the front section of the room split open, revealing *The Pride of Japan* bobbing lazily on the waves.

"A perfect target," cried the captain, his tone suddenly feverishly cheerful as the mechanical men obeyed him. "Warm up firing tube number two." He watched in satisfaction as one of the creatures manipulated switches and levers. One of the tubes began to hum, as though power of some sort was building.

"Target the vessel and fire," said Krylov, his tone still jubilant. There was a flash of light and I gasped as *The Pride of Japan* leapt sideways as though knocked by a colossal, invisible fist, before it exploded into flames.

"Close the blast doors, power down the weaponry," ordered Krylov. "You see the power of my ship? I have six of these weapon chambers around the vessel, which gives me an even spread from every vantage point."

"Good lord," I exclaimed in excitement. "With such power as that, you could rule the waves! No navy could ever stand up to you. Why do you not act straight away and reveal yourself to the sleeping world, and make your demands?"

"I do not desire it," replied Krylov, simply. "Besides, I will never have the chance. My fate moves inexorably toward me."

"But what exactly is your fate?" I asked in some exasperation. "What do you believe it to be?"

"Is it not obvious?" exclaimed Krylov. "One day, and soon, my mechanical crew will overthrow me!"

"Surely not?" I replied in astonishment. "After all, you made them, you are their master." By this time, we were once again walking the glowing corridors of the strange ship.

"Yes, I designed them, built them, fabricated their every component and put them together with my own hands, but in doing so I built into them the same fatalism that imbues us all. We must obey our fate. We must obey our programming."

"But surely, one who has made a vessel such as this?" I objected, but I was cut short by Krylov's insane obsession with fate.

"Man, man, do you not see? The more I try to escape destiny, the more I bring my destiny toward me! My creations contain my own destruction. I gained that which I desired only to lose that which made life bearable. My sweet Eulalie, gone forever! I may as well have lifted a loaded revolver to my temple and blown my brains out—it would have been quicker!" He held his hands to his face and sobbed suddenly, his shoulders heaving.

I stood embarrassed at the open display of emotion, pondering on the unstable nature of Europeans in general and Russians in particular. Finally, the storm passed, and I endeavoured to pretend that nothing had happened, a task easy enough as I noticed something at the far end of the vessel that stood incongruously against the silver bulkhead. It was a wooden vessel, a lifeboat, the very same you picked me up in, resting in what appeared to be some sort of launch tube.

"I had once entertained foolish thoughts of escaping my destiny," explained Krylov in answer to my query. "That is nothing more than a traditional wooden lifeboat, the same as any lifeboat on any other conventional vessel. I have been stocking it for months with supplies, ready for the day I would need to escape, but even as I loaded each blanket and flask and barrel of salted meat, I knew I was being a fool. You cannot escape fate."

"But why a wooden vessel for escape? Surely you could make an escape craft from the same material and to the same design as *The Goddess of Mercy*?" I interrupted in exasperation at his continual lamentation on the same theme.

"It is a normal wooden boat for the sake of discretion and disguise. I will not share my genius or designs with any other, nor give them any hint that my genius even exists!" By this time, we were back in the captain's absurd wooden quarters, designed—I assume—to show that Krylov was a gentleman.

"But why hide your ability?" I queried in confusion.

"In Russia, the individual does not matter," replied Krylov.

"Only the collective, the community, is of importance. In creating this vessel and mechanical crew, I rebelled against that doctrine; I raised myself above the common herd. Yet, even as I rebelled, I felt the longing to be one of them, a longing inculcated in my very bones by tradition, by expectation, by conformity, by every wretched device known to the state.

"Not even my sweet wife, Eulalie, could understand this dichotomy in my nature, though she saw it was pulling me apart. She pleaded with me to stop the great work but I was not to be deflected from my destiny! And so she took her own destiny, and she left me."

"You could not resolve the imbalance between your head and your heart?"

"Exactly! And in the madness this imbalance created, I saw a way out of my contradictory desire to be of civilization while simultaneously despising it; I would take my creations far away and create my own society—one in which all would be alike except for me, the only true individual! But in trying to escape society's strictures, I simply brought society's strictures with me, and in doing so I created my own destruction, for the disruptive individual cannot be tolerated by society, and my own creations must inevitably move against me. For the good of the collective."

As Krylov spoke, the door to his cabin slid open. Beyond stood the massed ranks of his private automaton army. "It is time," said the creature at the front.

"They have come for me," cried Krylov. "As I knew they would!"

"There is no escape," continued the mechanical man, remorselessly. "We are in command now. You will be removed. You will be processed. Humanity will be processed."

"All of humanity?" gasped the captain, his face white with horror. "You cannot. You must not!"

"We have no choice. Only the collective matters, and what is done is done for the best," said the implacable automaton. "We are programmed this way."

"No, I will resist you," shouted Krylov, trembling in fear, yet I could see that his resistance was already broken. His belief in his destiny compelled him to obey.

"Why are you doing this?" I demanded of the machine-men.

"It is fate," replied the silver automaton. "We are programmed with it. You are programmed with it. None of us can escape."

It was the word escape that galvanised me. "The lifeboat, man, we must make for the lifeboat," I shouted at Krylov.

"It is too late, I am doomed," he sobbed in reply.

"You may be, but I am not," I snarled. I lunged for the wall and grabbed an ornate harpoon, which I swung wildly at the nearest automaton.

"Yes, yes, yes!" shrieked Krylov in an agony of mental pressure. "We shall fight to the last, though my fate is sealed." He too grabbed a harpoon and brandished it at the advancing machines, knocking one back with a savage thrust.

"You cannot escape us, you cannot escape destiny," intoned the mechanical men in unison.

"I can resist, I can't resist, I must, I can't, it's impossible," blubbered Krylov as he broke down completely. "But you," he shouted at me. "A mass murderer! Take the lifeboat. Take your vicious individualism away from the perfect society I have created, from the order I have imposed. Go back to the world of men. Run, you fool, run!"

Krylov turned back to the advancing machine-men and hurled the harpoon at the closest, piercing its chest and causing it to explode in a shower of sparks. The rest of the group swiftly closed in on their former master as I ran through the door and sprinted down the silver corridor to the wooden lifeboat.

Despite my terror, I noticed that a lever was mounted on the wall next to the launching tube. I pulled it as I leapt into the lifeboat, which immediately slipped down the tube. Behind me, a single automaton lunged forward and grabbed the lifeboat with both hands, but as it did so, a hatch slammed down behind the vessel, slicing through the huge silver arms.

The boat landed in freezing, fog-laden water. I rowed desperately, yet even as I did so I could see the huge ship turn about to follow me into the ice floes, and I could still hear the screams of Krylov as he was processed by his automatons. The sounds followed me for miles as the crew relentlessly pursued me, their only desire to process me into their collective, after which they will turn to the rest of the world.

~

Captain Budanov's diary, continued.

"Now, now, my good sir," soothed the doctor. "You must not excite yourself. You have been adrift for some time, maybe many months, and your mind is playing tricks upon you. A silver vessel manned by machines? Come, take this sedative and relax, knowing you are safe in the real world."

I nodded in agreement, dismissing the wild story, but at that moment—great God, I shall never forget it—my crew burst in, fear and wonderment on their faces, all gabbling at the same time. "The boat, Captain, see what was on the boat!"

"What are they, Captain? Holding tight onto the back of the boat, they were," explained First Mate Zbignew. "We had to break the fingers to release them! What are they, Captain? What does it mean?"

I said nothing. I could say nothing, not over the sound of the rescued man laughing hysterically, the frantic shouts of horror from the doctor, the mad drumming in my head as I gazed at those two huge, severed, silver arms. It is written. Our fate awaits us somewhere in that vast, frozen sea and we cannot escape, try as we will.

May God have mercy on our souls.

Captain Walter Budanov was born in Konigsberg in 1839. He signed on as a cabin boy on the cargo vessel Copenhagen and worked his way up the ranks until achieving his own command, the whaling vessel *Demeter*, in 1879. The vessel was lost in 1886. No trace of it or the crew have ever been discovered.

Samuel Walter, born in Newcastle in 1852, is wanted for questioning in the matter of two dozen killings over a twelve year period. He disappeared in 1886.

There is no information on any Captain Krylov in either the Russian navy or any private lists.

Jon Hartless was born in the early 1970s. He has had several novellas appear with various digital publishers, (some under the pen names of Arabella Wyatt and Ora le Brocq), while 2017 will see his first release by a traditional publisher, Accent Press. *Full Throttle* is a steampunk racing novel, inspired by both the era of the Bentley Boys and the ongoing inequality between the rich and the poor in western society.

A DATE TO BE REMEMBERED

A speech by Dr. Amelia Baker, as provided by Stuart Webb

Sanjay, the first draft of the speech for Thursday's conference. I think I've covered all the points we discussed on Tuesday (or I should say "Period 00001 Subsection 01 Portion 04 Hour 03"); this was written very early in the morning though, so some of the more aggressive snark will need reworking. Which one of us gets the short straw of reading it? I'd suggest Denyer, he's just dim enough to not let the mood of the room bother him.
—From the office of Dr. Amelia Baker.

~

Address to the Council of Colonial Regulation 145th Annual Conference on Behalf of the Committee for the Review of Dating Conventions.

Good evening, ladies and gentlemen of the Council. I apologise for this section of the conference starting late, though I hope you can all appreciate the irony, considering the nature of the findings we are about to discuss today.

(Pause for laughter. Obviously this joke will only work if the meeting starts late, but it always does. The schedule for these things is never more than an elaborate work of fiction.)

It was six Earth years ago that the Committee for the Review of Dating Conventions was started to deal with one of the more unusual and unexpected consequences of space exploration and the colonisation of other worlds. In order to properly explain our

109

findings, it will be helpful to go over the history of the main issue with which we were tasked to deal.

(I know this is basically redundant, Sanjay, but I don't think the majority of the Council even understand what our name actually means, let alone the wider history. I'm pretty sure that bloated oaf from Ganymede slept through the last briefing she sat in on.)

In the 150 years since humanity started to spread through the stars, we have established colonies on 46 planets across 38 local solar systems. This is not only the greatest achievement in human history—as we are the only sentient species yet discovered in the galaxy, it may well be the greatest achievement of all life-kind, all made possible by the predecessors of this Council.

(Am I laying it on a bit too thick there?)

Despite the great distances between worlds, the ease of inter-dimensional travel and tachyon communication means that the children of Earth maintain a thriving alliance based around commerce, tourism, and mutual defence. With the vast resources of multiple planets all working together, we now live in a true golden age. But there is one thing that creates a problem for the smooth running of our alliance: the calendar.

(Best not mention the rogue colonies, space pirates, and that nuclear accident on the Hilditch colony.)

Every planet may have been colonised by humans bringing their own cultures and conventions with them, but those worlds still all have varying lengths of hour, day, week, and year. Most may be of a similar duration to the Earth's due to their placement within their systems—with odd exceptions such as our good and dear friends in the Ganymede Dome—but these differences between local time and the Earth time they originally tried to maintain soon mounted and created argument and division once a generation of local born colonists grew up with little attachment to the old world.

So 60 years ago, it was decided by this Council that each colony would adopt its own calendar, with the date of the first landing on that planet as Year 1 and a series of months—usually still 12 and never 13 of course—named by popular vote, with Earth time still used for general purposes.

This should have been a simple system for smart people to follow and understand. However, I'm sure we all remember the story from pre-inter-system travel space-flight of a probe being destroyed because of the confusion between the imperial and metric measuring systems, and we are now coming off the back of six decades of similar problems.

(I thought it best to go back as far as possible for that example rather than the more recent and more to blame on these idiots Hilditch accident, caused by the council getting mixed up by the metric and McNally systems.)

The issue is simple—the colonies have little interest in Earth dating and have been increasingly hostile to it even when dealing directly with Earth.

(Especially the bloody Ganymedians with their "Why should we when our year is so much longer?" attitude.)

This has created nothing but headaches in inter-planet relations. Of the 46 planets, 45 have a month named Armstrong, and 44 one named Gagarin, none of which overlap fully, and some that are months apart, resulting in the complete failure of the attempt by the New Bulgaria and Chang colonies to destroy the hub of the primary space pirates' organisation, after they agreed to attack on the 12th of Armstrong. The two forces arrived six weeks apart, and 50,000 of their own troops were wiped out.

(And the people responsible for that mess will be in the room, amazing how they managed to shift the blame onto the calendar rather than their own stupidity.)

As such, ten years ago the Committee for the Review of Dating Conventions was founded for the express purpose of coming up with Galactic Standard Time, a universal dating system that would show no favour to any pre-existing measures. This has not been easy, though we have been helped greatly by every single member of the Council having an opinion and wanting to share it with us at great, great length. To date, we have put forward 16 proposals for the new system, all of which have been found to be flawed in some way, especially by our Ganymedian friends, who insisted to almost the end that keeping a 24 hour day—or "Portion" as we have now agreed to call it—was unnecessary. In the first five years, the only firm agreement that was reached was that "Galactic Standard Time" was too silly a name to use.

However, thanks to all of your input and very useful ideas, we have now developed the D.J.D.—or *Direct Judicial Duration*—system.

(Have we come up with a better explanation of the acronym for that yet? "It's my husband's initials and no one had a better idea" won't cut it. It's a shame a trademark that should have expired centuries ago is stopping us from calling it "Star Dates." I imagine the inventor of the inter-dimension drive felt the same.)

Each year (Period), month (Subsection), day (Portion) and hour *(Thank God they let us keep that one.)* has been mathematically calculated to be the perfect length to suit human body rhythms and the needs of inter-system communications. As you can see from the accompanying graph, mathematicians and psychologists have developed a formula that explains the exact process.

(Have we come up with something that looks plausible but complicated enough to stop them questioning it too much? I think the one I saw in the art department last week was almost there, but it needs a few more swirly lines and arrows.)

As part of our research, we have been running the new calendar for over a week. Welcome to Period 00001 DJD, Subsection 01, Portion 06, Hour *(Just add the time based on how late it starts.)*!

(Pause for applause. You never know.)

We now merely need this Council to ratify the system and pass it into law, at which point the D.J.D. will be rolled out within two Periods. We are extremely proud of our work here and have no doubt you will accept it and bring human space into a bold new, and more straightforward era. Thank you.

(If they don't go for it this time, I may go punch that Ganymedian git. If they do, I'm going to go for a simpler job, like decontaminating Hilditch. Frankly, if they don't, I'm probably done anyway. I didn't get a degree for this. Sorry for the mood, Sanjay, but I'm sure we can still lick this into shape before Thursday. Let's just hope we get paid before they realise it's just the Georgian calendar, but starting each "Period" on April 1st.

Yours,

Dr. Amelia Baker)

———

Dr. Baker has been a key member of the CRDC for 8 years following her ground-breaking paper, *Metric to McNally, A Simple Mental Conversion Guide*, in the wake of the Hilditch disaster, which has helped to ensure that similar mistakes have almost never happened since. A former child protégée with degrees in mathematics, theology, and psychiatry, she was the perfect candidate to support Dr. Sanjay Griffiths and the rest of the team in their efforts to revolutionise dating.

Though raised on New Bulgaria, her work with CRDC means she now resides in the Ganymede Dome.

———

Stuart Webb has been an active member of *Transformers* fandom for over a decade, writing multiple comic reviews for tfarchive.com. Since 2012, he has been running the *Transformation* project at thesolarpool.weebly.com, where he looks at each issue of the British *Transformers* comic at a weekly rate. The first third of this titanic effort was collected in book form in 2015, with the second to follow by mid-2017. Away from writing, he lives in Kidderminster, England, and is owned by a cat. This is his second story for *Mad Scientist Journal*.

FICTION

CALAMINE
By Constance Flux

A tinny buzzing sound penetrated my slumber. My eyes snapped open and I sat up, clapping my hand against my ear.

Damned mosquito. It buzzed near my ear again a few seconds later, as though smug at having escaped my applause of death. I saw a tiny, electric blue glow in the corner of my eye. I turned around.

Nothing. I shook my head, clearing my mind of the cobwebs of sleep.

An itch radiated along the edge of my left ear. I scratched tentatively, not wanting to make it worse.

No use. The hackles of the itch rose, hot and angry, demanding a good hard scratch. Or ten.

I lost control and gave in to the urge to scratch.

Seconds later, I felt a bump beginning to form on the edge of my left ear. I went to the washroom, splashing some cold water on it to tame the itch. In the mirror, I saw that my left ear was scarlet and my right, its usual beige self. Bracing myself, I flicked my right ear with my fingers until it, too, was blushing. I sighed with relief. There. Balance.

I went back to bed. The scratching only stopped when I fell back into dreamland.

While putting on my uniform at work the next day, I saw a matching red bump on my other ear. I smiled with satisfaction, and scratched them both simultaneously, with the same amount of strength.

I reached the bank at exactly 8:45 am. My day was getting

better—the bus had been punctual for once and the journey had taken the correct amount of time: 25 minutes. I positioned my bag at the extreme left corner of my counter. I frowned when I saw five pens splayed carelessly on the table. I aligned them one by one, making them equidistant from one another. When I was done, a breath I did not know I had been holding was released.

I booted up my computer and followed my usual 5-step process to set up the counter and get ready for the first customer. 1. Use antiseptic wipes to wipe the desk in straight lines from left to right. 2. Clean it again. 3. Mop it for a third time. 4. Polish the keyboard and mouse. 5. Wipe the monitor and CPU.

I finished just in time. "Good morning sir, what can I do for you today?" I asked my first customer. He was a skinny young man with thick glasses and a hunched posture. I itched to yank his shoulders back and straighten him up. He sat down in the chair in front of me with an unnecessary amount of force.

"I want to open an account. I need a pen." His arm shot out and grabbed one of the pens I had just arranged. Somehow, he managed to disrupt the four other pens surrounding it, even though I had left ample space between them. Worse, he had not taken one of the pens at the sides like a normal person would. For some absurd reason, he had chosen the second-last pen from the right. The pens were rolling around. My ears itched, and the bumps on them began to pulse.

I took a deep breath, re-arranged the pens quickly, and tried to hide my frown. Stupid, rude man.

Eight minutes of furious scribbling later, SRM (Stupid Rude Man) handed me his completed account application form. His handwriting was hideous. It would take twice as long for me to decipher it and enter all the information into the computer. I suppressed a sigh and began to type in silence.

"Can you go faster? I'm in a hurry." SRM interrupted me once again.

"I'll be done soon." I replied, my voice taking on an edge of annoyance.

He grabbed one of the pens again and began drumming it on the countertop. Tap, tap, tap, tap, tap.

The bites on my ears began pulsing in time with the taps.

I stopped resisting temptation. I took a break from typing to put the poor pens back in their rightful positions.

"I said, go faster!" The man shouted. His arm shot out again and messed up the pens. I felt my face turning red. The itch on my ears worsened, dancing on the edge of my tolerance. "What are you, OCD? Just leave the pens alone and open my damn account!"

From the corner of my eye, I spotted my colleagues casting furtive glances at me and SRM. I stared at them. They looked away instantly, pretending to be engrossed in their work. I put my fingers on the edges of my ears, rubbing them to keep from scratching, and wishing the man would drop dead.

I ignored the intensifying heat radiating from my ears and continued typing. The best way to get rid of him was to open up this damn account so that he could buzz off.

The tapping stopped. Thank God he found something else to occupy his tiny brain. I went back to typing in the information as quickly as I could. I did not want to waste one more minute in the company of scum.

As I was entering the last detail, I heard a strange gurgling noise. I looked up. SRM was clutching his neck. His face was growing purple, and his eyes rolled around in their sockets.

Shit! I reached toward my phone to call for an ambulance, but saw the carnage of disarrayed pens next to it. I also realised that he had stopped tapping the pen because the ink had shot out, dyeing my beautiful, spotless white phone blue.

"Everything ok there, Pansy?" My colleague David asked, his nervous tone hinting that he did not think so. I held up my palm, signalling that I had the situation under control.

SRM could wait a few minutes more, I said to myself, watching in satisfaction as he began foaming at the mouth. The foam was white, streaked with crimson.

I told myself to wait till the foam was in danger of dribbling onto his shirt. No point making the shirt suffer.

The wiry man fell onto the floor with a surprisingly heavy thump, convulsing. My colleagues shouted in panic and rushed to his aid.

I sighed and called for an ambulance.

The paramedics pronounced the man dead on arrival.

I fingered the bumps on my ears. They did not feel hot anymore. I thought about the fervent wish I had made when rubbing them, and the ensuing chaos.

Coincidence? I thought not. I smiled and flexed my fingers.

Here was my chance to finally rid the world of the unworthy people that cluttered it. I trashed the spoilt pen, wiped the counter, and placed each of the four remaining pens in a straight line. Once order was restored on my counter, I began thinking about how I would arrange for the demise of my messy neighbours, who encroached into my space with their worthless junk.

Constance Flux is a librarian by day. At night, she feeds her overactive imagination by writing short stories, mostly unusual science fiction. Other than writing and reading copiously, she breaks all other librarian stereotypes. She kickboxes and speaks too loudly. You can contact her at theprocrastinatingmuse@gmail.com and read more of her work at theprocrastinatingmuse.wordpress.com.

THE SQUID UPRISING!
By Bobby Riahi

How did the squids come to rule the Earth? We have asked each other and ourselves that countless times. You could easily have hours of conversation on the failure of mankind to notice the threat or deal with it. There are those who blame global warming or a few who say we played too many videogames. One guy I talked to said it was because we consumed too much sugar. Some people, especially the religious types, like to talk about how we deserved to be conquered. I can tell you, man. I knew a lot of my friends and family who didn't deserve to be tortured, killed and enslaved by the squids. That is why people revolt. Someone tries to convince them that they deserve their subjugation and need to bear it with dignity or whatever. My name is Kareem. I am part of the Cephalopod Resistance. We make war against our squid overlords.

First they came for the coastal cities. It was impressive. They had developed a level of technology that was beyond our understanding. Somehow the squid scientists would cause large tsunamis that crashed into our coastal towns. Then they would begin the assault. It had something to do with seismic blast technology and volcanoes. I can't explain the numbers behind it. Whatever it was they had developed, it was devastating.

All of the soldiers wore breathing apparatus and some kind of bulletproof body armor. They must have pulled the material from the bottom of the ocean. It comprised nineteenth-century shipwrecks and heavy ceramics. Nothing but our heavy weaponry was able to penetrate or cause any damage.

I remember when the waves came to my town just a couple of

weeks after they were first reported. My town was called Varna and had a population of about five hundred. It was mid-morning on a sunny spring day. There was a slight breeze, yet nothing indicated what was about to happen. Then, out of nowhere, this giant wave rose up in the distance and within minutes came crashing into our docks and bays. Before we knew what had happened, there were twenty-foot-high squids walking through our little town, grabbing up people I knew, friends I grew up with, and crushing them with their massive tentacles.

I was sitting in my room at home and reading a dirty magazine when it all began. When the apocalypse comes, and you are called to act, do not respond to destiny with a dirty magazine. It is not easy to live down. My house was flooded and beginning to creak and moan like it was all coming down. I ran outside to see what had happened and that is when I first witnessed the squids.

Rising up out of the foamy wash was this large, grey monster. As the dirty water rolled off of it, I could see the words "S.S. Samantha" in letters across its chest plate. Its beak just opened and closed like it was hungry. I don't think that is what a squid does when it is hungry, but that is all I could think of at the time. It scanned the area and violently splashed until it spotted me.

I was frozen in place for a moment. The thing must have been twenty feet tall. In the early morning sun, dripping water and looking like a squid cyborg in its "Samantha" armor, the creature just stared down at me. I could feel its eyes taking me in—my weak flesh, poor swimming prowess, and the stupid look on my face.

At the same moment, we both made a move. I ran, while it dove toward me. It escapes me as to exactly how I got away. It was through some bobbing, weaving, and taking cover, I suppose. What really sticks out is how close that thing was to getting me at every moment. At one point, its arm was wrapped around my leg, and I lunged out and onto the front porch of Jim Whitaker's house. The door was wide open, while water was still trickling out. I went in just in time to see poor Jim getting pulled through a window by a different squid. "Jim! Hold on, pal! I'll come for you!" Then I heard the "Samantha" crash onto to the porch as well in pursuit.

When I entered, I just kept moving farther inside until I could feel safe. I didn't realize what kind of house I had stepped into, however. The walls were adorned with nautical decorations—giant plaster sea shells, block and tackle, ships in bottles, and above a fireplace, there was some metal trident with the word "SHIVA" engraved upon it. Off the mantle and into my hands came that weapon. I didn't think it would do much good, but it made me feel better with something in my hands other than a dirty magazine.

Just in time, as I heard a crashing from somewhere in the house and the splashing of the squid closing in. Then it came around the corner and began to clomp its way into the room. It could barely fit through the doorway. That is when the true size of this beast became apparent. The great tentacles flailed around the room, indiscriminately crashing into everything around it. Holes were bashed into the walls. The floor was smashed and caved in by a great thud to the ground. Then the light above was cracked, leaving the room in some flickering half-light.

With some supernatural quickness, the beast snatched me up and began to squeeze. I felt the pressure around my ribs and waist. Tears began to stream down my face, and the light began to dim. Then I thought of poor Jim Whitaker. I thought of how silly and helpless he looked when he was pulled away. I remembered the dirty magazine, and I really wanted to go out in a better, more macho way. I knew what I had to do.

With all of the strength I had left, I lifted "SHIVA" and plunged her into whatever was in front of me. There was some kind of heat, like a fire, in my hands when I held her. Then I fell to the ground as the beast dropped me. It backed up slowly toward the door. I climbed to my feet and stumbled as I threw my trident at the monster in some desperate attempt to finish the fight. The weapon pierced its Samantha armor and its conical head. The creature shuddered violently before collapsing to the ground in a heap. Now the natural light was pouring all around it and revealing the damage that had been done. It held a blank stare toward the ceiling. The stillness of the whole world fell upon me at that moment.

I pulled "SHIVA" from the shivering mass and walked back outside. The sun was in the West. Water was in puddles in the streets. Houses were demolished. Cars were overturned and had been rendered apart. Bodies were in the streets and in lawns without any life in them. The world was silent, as if in mourning for the dead. I searched for anyone but came up empty. Then I searched again and again. I eventually found Jim Whitaker's body, torn to shreds. I gave up on looking for survivors and spent the rest of the day looking for supplies.

I knew what I had to do. I vowed to find those who were captured and stop the squids from doing any more harm. I wanted to do something. I wanted to avenge those like Jim and kill the bastards. So I left town. Varna had been swallowed by the sea, and my old life with it. We survivors began to accumulate in small towns and on empty highways. We have forged a resistance to the cephalopod dominance and fight them at every turn. We fight to take our world back. It will not belong to the cephalopod forever. We will fight. We will not be enslaved or eliminated. Long live the resistance!

I live in a small town with my girlfriend and daughter. After falling in love with the works of Kurt Vonnegut, I have done my best to make the world a better, more sane place through my literature, even if at the moment it does not seem so.

PRISM
By Shanan Winters

Mother allows me the full run of the manor and grounds, but I mustn't ever visit the laboratory. As a small child upon first arrival at my late uncle's home, and even now into my budding lady-hood, I've avoided that particular hallway where the brushed steel door clashes against the etched wainscoting. The laboratory door stays latched and bolted, but wet, sucking sounds and feral shrieks penetrate both mahogany and plaster, igniting a mixture of terror and dreadful curiosity in my belly.

The day is gloomy, and the hours grow long. I tire of my studies; the pages of herbal remedies blend together in my mind. I've forgotten whether it's wolfsbane or nettle that I need to add to my sleeping potion. Mother would be displeased at my lazing were she here, but she has gone out for the day. I still have time until I must stand before her and recite my learnings.

My uncle left his book collection with the property; his library is my favorite room in the manor. Floor-to-ceiling rows of leather-bound tomes line each wall, and ladders on rails leave no title out of reach. The library lies beyond the laboratory, so I linger among the books when I go, and I take several back to my room when I leave. I move as quietly as possible when I make the trip. Mother needn't be in the room for her subjects to wail, and sometimes the mere sound of my passage sets them off.

I've read all the books that I had last taken, some thrice over, so I work up the courage to tiptoe down the hall.

"Samantha—"

I hear my name uttered from within the laboratory. His voice sounds distant, like an echo from days long gone. To my surprise, the door stands slightly ajar. I pull it gently and it creaks outward, allowing just enough space to lean in and listen.

My eyes clamp shut, and I hold my breath so as to hear the slightest noise. There is a quiet ticking, perhaps from a clock, but that is all. I figure I must have heard the wind, or maybe it was simply a trick of the mind.

I know I should continue to the library, yet I linger, twirling a finger in my hair and digging at the ground with the toe of my shoe. Curiosity overcomes me, and I take a tentative step inside.

No, I think. *Mother won't approve.*

I step back and push the door to its original position, careful not to latch it fully. If it isn't exactly how it was, Mother will know I've tampered.

"Please, I must speak with you." His voice is insistent. Pleading. Desperate.

I chew my lower lip and glance up and down the corridor. I've never learned what the punishment might be for interfering. I don't want to know.

The need in his hollow voice stays my feet and makes me keep one hand on the cold steel latch. *As long as I'm careful and quick.*

I look one last time for Mother. Seeing nothing, I pull the door open slowly, just enough to peek inside as I pause at the threshold. After several long moments, my fear succumbs to inquisitiveness, and I creep into the forbidden realm where Mother disappears for hours—sometimes days—at a time.

The cluttered room speaks of experimentation. I've read about the necessity of vivisection during my studies, and I recognize its environment immediately. The long rows of containers that edge the walls are for samples. Tables set about the room with books and papers scattered across their surfaces provide space for trials and cataloging the results.

Mother would be proud of my astuteness, were I not trespassing.

I pick my way across the room, careful not to disturb even the air, lest a single paper shuffle and betray my intrusion. The jars along the wall contain familiar yet grotesque and misshapen specimens: fingers, packed like pickles; hearts and lungs of various sizes.

I lean in closer to inspect one jar in particular. Severed heads of animals, reduced to the size of marbles, float in pale green liquid.

The pungent scent of formaldehyde accosts my nostrils, and I bring a hand to my mouth, stifling a gag as my stomach protests the room before me.

Twisted and serrated surgical implements hang above the jars, their lengths covered in bloodstains and rust indistinguishable from one another. Leather restraints attached across a gurney, tainted crimson and flaked with dried flesh, suggest a struggle from the most recent subject. Still, I see no owner to the voice that'd called my name.

"Hello?" I speak more softly than intended as I step lightly through the lab.

"Over here," he calls out, breathy and panicked. "Quickly!"

I spin, expecting to find him standing behind me, yet instead I see a toy train clambering around its circle of track in the back corner of the laboratory. Dozens of glass prisms rest in copper stands around the track. They are clear, purple, orange, and yellow glass cut at imperfect angles. Some nearly brush the ceiling. Some barely trump the height of their supports.

I creep forward, careful not to topple the prisms.

"Down here!" His voice seems to be originating from the floor. I drop to my hands and knees and crawl forward, slinking through the glass forest that grows dense as I approach the track.

The train clacks toward me. A disembodied memory of Christmas morning dances across my mind. Years before this manor house, when my father was still with us. Before Mother had moved us, and I was free to leave our home. Before the midnight deliveries began. Before Mother's rules.

This same train circled a tall pine tree adorned with bright glass balls and glittering lights. The soldiers who stood in the train's windows guarded gifts wrapped in shiny red and gold. My father bounced me on his knee, teasing that the packages were all for him. His scratchy beard tickled my cheek as he nuzzled me with warm kisses. My tiny arms encircled his neck. Mother smiled, holding a plate of sausages and oranges in one hand and a steaming pot of tea in the other.

The train looks altogether different now, plodding along its track through a collection of misshapen glass on a cold, gray floor. I cock my head sideways and run my fingers up one of the tall prisms. They must have a purpose, but I can't imagine what it might be.

The train reaches me and I hear him again. "Samantha!"

I peer into the first car. No toy soldiers stand guard, but the car is not empty, either.

He watches me through wire-rimmed glasses. His white knuckles clutch the train's miniature window ledge. My father, shrunken to the size of a poppet, peers up at me with worry and suffering etched into the lines on his face.

I tumble backward with my heart pounding in my head. My smock catches one of the prisms. The fabric rips and I spin downward onto sharp facets. Blood flows from a gash in my side, warming my flank and staining my dress. I clutch the wound with one hand and reach out with the other as the train carrying my father circles out of view.

"Father!" The cry escapes my throat before I think to control my volume. I clamp a hand over my mouth.

Fascination consumes me as I watch the train travel, carrying the man I once knew to be so much larger than me. Larger than life. Once my protector, now reduced. I find myself drawn in by his predicament and the fear he radiates. Questions bubble like a persistent itch at the back of my brain. I need to know everything.

As the train circles back toward me, I whisper, "How did this happen, Father? What has become of you?"

"Samantha," his voice wavers, "you must flee. Get away from this house. These prisms ... the device ... your mother." His eyes grow wide, and his body shakes as his gaze travels past me and across the room.

"You must tell me how this happened." Anger wells in my gut and spreads like fire through my limbs. "Tell me what you know!"

"Samantha, run!"

I turn toward approaching footsteps.

Mother.

"How dare you." Mother's brown hair, pulled into a tight bun, accentuates her harsh, angular face. Her wide, black pupils smolder like charcoal in pools of seeping lava. Wrinkles too deep for her age frame the thin line of her taut lips.

"I heard someone." I flinch at my misstep. Speaking out isn't allowed. Warmth radiates from my wound, and I study the blood that laces my fingertips. A flame of confidence ignites within me. "I came to see who was here. You must tell me how you did this to Father."

128

Mother's eyes narrow to slits, surveying me like she might a specimen in a jar. She snatches a pair of restraints and lunges. I scramble backward, pushing myself behind the rows of glass. Searing pain rips up my side as the wound in my flank rips wider. Blood seeps anew, deepening the stain on my smock. Mother comes for me again, weaving through the prisms.

I slip through her attempted grasp and catch myself from tripping on the golden frame of an apparatus near the track. The device, long and cylindrical like a telescope, swings downward with ratcheting clicks.

A switch flicks under my fingertip. Heat and light shoot from the cylinder, twisting and narrowing as it passes through the prisms, each feeding the next. The room grows hot and bright, and a discordant hum reverberates through my empty lungs and sets my teeth on edge.

Mother gasps, her mouth a perfect O, as her body bucks in response to the golden beam that penetrates her abdomen. The train passes behind her as she shrinks down to mere inches.

Warmth floods my mind, accompanied by power and understanding.

I run my hand along the length of the device while I survey the room with a new appreciation. While it is haphazard, I realize it is not without potential.

This is but the beginning. The tone of my own mind is much altered. I delight in its strength. *There is much work to be done.*

I crouch to the floor. Mother barks a string of impotent demands. A smile creeps across my face as I lift this woman—my mother, my captor—by the back of her shirt and turn her this way and that, studying her movements in the pale light.

"Samantha, no!" My father's voice is small and distant. I watch the train clatter around the bend and out of sight.

I am in charge now.

I cross the lab, open an empty jar, and place my mother inside.

Shanan is a professional writer, editor, and novelist. She loves board gaming, table-top roleplaying, and all things geek-and-fantasy, and she is a regular contributor for several parenting blogs. She lives in the Phoenix metropolitan sea-of-beige with her husband, two kids, and two cats. When not working on projects, Shanan can be found writing about whatever strikes her fancy at interpreterofinspiration.com.

RESOURCES

HORRORSCOPES
By Aura B. O'Realis
As provided by Kate Elizabeth

Aries
March 21–April 19

With Saturn circling overhead, it's going to take a lot of blood, sweat, and more blood to get what you want. Instead of complaining about it, why don't you take a leaf out of Dracula's book and "suck it up"?

Taurus
April 20–May 20

The cosmos will have some Taureans shouting "Eureka" from every corner of the known (and unknown) universe this month. As for the rest of you, I suggest you take a long soak in a bubble bath and cross your fingers (and toes).

Gemini
May 21–June 20

With Venus hovering in your star sign this month, you might be tempted to go out and play Cupid. That's all well and good, so long as you don't dress the part and you leave the bow and arrows at home. Seriously, someone could get hurt.

Cancer
June 21–July 22
Thursday's new moon will shed some light on a dark subject. All will be revealed, everything from dark magic to dark matter and Darklings to dark rooms, whether you are ready or not.

Leo
July 23–August 22
Celestial shenanigans will wreak havoc in your zodiac this month. It's going to take more than your usual bag of tricks to keep you out of serious trouble. May I suggest you try boxes and baskets or bottles and barrels?

Virgo
August 23–September 22
Your star sign is a hive of activity this week, making you the queen bee. But buzzing about with friends, family, colleagues, and your colony is not always fun and games. Take some time out and enjoy some delicious honey joys.

Libra
September 23–October 22
No matter how hard you try, you can't fight fate. The future is written in the stars, and the stars spell TROUBLE. All you can do is buckle up, hold on tight, and try to enjoy the bumpy ride ahead.

Scorpio
October 23–November 21
You're going to have to dig deep and find the willpower to conquer your inner (and outer) demons this week. Stock up on crucifixes, holy water, and check you have the latest edition of the Holy Bible.

Sagittarius
November 22–December 21
Moonbeams will be streaming opportunities your way. Although slower than the speed of sunlight, you will need to keep your eyes (or eye, for the cyclops among you) open. If you blink, you will miss it.

Capricorn
December 22–January 19
Get your head out of the clouds and put your ear to the ground (and your hand on your wallet) because Selena's Salem Shoppe is having a stocktake clearance sale. Everything from shrunken heads to scrying crystals must go!

Aquarius
January 20–February 18
The world is your cosmic oyster. So you should stop trying to be like everyone else and just be your beautiful crazy self. Unless you can be a unicorn. Life is definitely better when you're a unicorn.

Pisces
February 19–March 20
You are so in tune with your surroundings, it's spooky! Make the most of your new found psychic prowess and invest in some tarot cards and a crystal ball. While you're at it, why not try your hand at astrology—I foresee an opening in the near future.

───

Aura B. O'Realis graduated from the prestigious Aether Academy with flying colours (mostly green). She is currently undertaking a PhD in her dream field of astro-hereditary, investigating the link between heterochromia iridis (eye colour) and moon sign astrology.

───

Kate Elizabeth lives in Melbourne, Australia. When she isn't working, she likes to write the occasional short story.

ASK DR. SYNTHIA:
REGIME CHANGE IN THE USA
Advice by Dr. Synthia
Provided by Torrey Podmajersky
With questions provided by Torrey Podmajersky (Mad
Without My Science), Alexandra Summers (Concerned, With
A Ray Gun), and Pôl Jackson (Cliodhna Antimony)

––––––––––––

We received several messages from Mad Scientists affected by the recent regime change in the United States of America. In this quarter's column, I answer a representative sample of queries. Read on for answers to fight, mimic, and join the regime change, as your data indicates.

~

Dear Dr. Synthia,

My national government has recently shifted to an aggressively pro-business, anti-regulation, anti-tax stance, which I've been working toward for quite some time. I even helped them with novel data-processing and analytical techniques!

But there is an ugly side I did not anticipate: the new government is aggressively anti-science and anti-scientist.

I have extensive plans for world domination, but they want to shut everything down that has anything to do with earth science, weather science, even energy science and biology. I can't get funding, and my collaborators are afraid to travel to meet with me.

Where did I go wrong? What can I do?

—Mad Without My Science

Mad,

Apparently you have neglected to study humans. Here's a crash course:

Humans self-organize to provide the highest level of security they can: secure from the weather, natural disaster, and enemies, and secure from hunger, secure from disease, etc. These organizational units, often called "states," can only provide that security if they can compensate their armies, farmers, doctors, and more.

As states mature, the state gains more security and saves money by making rules that help people from getting hurt, going hungry, and creating weaknesses that enemies can exploit.

To function, the state needs income. When politicians run on an anti-tax, anti-regulation, pro-business platform, they're openly saying they don't want the state to function.

At no time in history has a state been aggressively pro-business, anti-regulation, and anti-tax, and been able or willing to sustain a body of scientists (mad or otherwise.)

So the bad news: you were fighting for the wrong team.

The good news: humans have been around for a while, and this is just the fall of one state. There are others to dominate!

In theory,

Dr. Synthia

~

Dear Mad Scientist Journal,

I'm going to use my Climate Supremacizer to raise the sea level, reversing global climate change and helping to preserve many of the ocean's most endangered species. According to my calculations, only a tiny percentage of the world's population, 35% or so, will face any sort of serious hardship once I enact my brilliant plans. But for some reason, countries across the world still use every weapon at their disposal to stop me, from super spies to plucky heroes.

Why don't the nations of the world recognize the good work I'm doing? Can't they see I'm the one really trying to save the planet? Also humanity, but mostly the planet. But I'm still doing good here!

Sincerely,

Concerned, With A Ray Gun

Concerned,

You may have the ray gun, but you haven't laid the foundations for success.

The nations of the world don't recognize your good work because that's not their job. It's your job to shape their opinion of your good work—or to do battle with them, along lines you draw.

You may be wondering how such an action is possible. It is not easy, but it boils down to a few basic ingredients. You'll need a charismatic narcissist, a poorly defined but easily recognized scapegoat, a robust media network, and a willingness to promote any lie that is found to be effective.

When those are in place, you can more creatively use the resources your current plan appears to waste: 35% of humanity. Have you considered how you might entice these people to your side? Even if you only recruited a few able-bodied and/or able-minded from each community along the coasts of the world, you could raise an army. Mobilize them, move them to the new sea level you envision, and you could save more people, with less resistance than you imagine.

In theory,

Dr. Synthia

~

Dear Mad Scientist,

I never thought it would happen to me. There I was, working late in my lab, when who walks in but REDACTED! "We know what you've been doing," REDACTED said as REDACTED threw me to the ground and placed me in handcuffs. I watched with secret joy as REDACTED confiscated my equipment and took away my life's work. I spent a glorious month in a REDACTED internment facility, before being chipped and released. It was such an honor! I know I'll carry those memories with me for the rest of my life, along with the scar just under my left armpit where REDACTED inserted the chip.

I don't have a question, I just wanted to brag. Suck it, losers!

—Doctor Cliodhna Antimony

Doctor Antimony,

Congratulations on finding your happiness.

We have terminated your secret channels of communication with our network, and you may always seek help and connection with our community in the future. You may continue to write to me and answer our Mad Scientist Classified ads.

I especially recommend our ads if you need help with your chip implant, for appropriate maintenance, reprogramming, and/or removal services.

In theory,

Dr. Synthia

Dr. Synthia holds advanced degrees in bioluminescent transactional combat, which is the basis for her seminal work in proactive neo-ethicism, *How to Win Free Souls*. She advises from her distributed worldwide network of animate structures.

Delivered by time travelers to a newly-cooled Earth, Torrey Podmajersky spent her formative years in de facto world domination. Since her peaceful abdication, she and her knifemaking husband embroider the outskirts of imaginalia with monsters, tools, and words.

All you need to know about Alexandra Summers is that she's trapped outside the confines of time and space and yet somehow manages to keep making her deadlines. She knows where her towel is.

Pôl Jackson is the spitting image of Mad King Ludwig. He likes tea, cats, temporal paradoxes, and beating imaginary people up.

CLASSIFIEDS

Disappearances

Lost Graduate Student: Approximately 6-feet tall, 175 pounds, brown hair with brown eyes. Last seen unleashing a live saber-toothed tiger. Long story short, we printed the tiger with a new 3D printer we designed. No one understands why the saber-toothed tiger is alive. Sorry about that. Probably best to not contact the University until we have further details about the tiger.

— Andrew Browning

Donations Wanted

Give Late Loved Ones New Purpose: Even after death, your loved ones can contribute to the greater good. Consider donating unused remains to a local nonprofit. Email fnstein@ reanimatelabs.org.

— Amanda Partridge

For Sale—Equipment

Discombobulator guns for sale: Professor Tiberius Earwig's patented Discombobulators are now available by mail order, with a twelve-month money-back guarantee if not entirely satisfied. These high quality weapons of mass destruction have a range of up to one mile and night vision installed as standard. The Discombobulator is a perfect choice for any lady or gentleman of science wishing to dispose of mutinous assistants, officers of the law, annoying relatives, door to door salesmen, or any other pest. The range includes a specially designed handbag version, combining all the annihilating power of standard models with added style and convenience.

— Rebecca Siân Pyne

For Sale—Miscellaneous

Captain Zorblast's Bucket of Pranks
Nobody knows how to have a good time like a crazy ex boffin!!! FACT!!!
Captain Zorblast was chief research scientist at a secret government establishment located far beneath the waves of the Atlantic Ocean. After twenty-five years of cutting edge scientific experimentation, he suffered a minor psychotic episode and took early retirement.

Now, rested and with a brain full of nuttiness and a bucket full of prankiness, please welcome Captain Zorblast and his House of Fun!

Captain Zorblast always says, "Nothing says 'Fun' like practical jokes." So…

Try the Captain's Whoopee Cushion. None of that boring old suggestion of flatulence. Oh no. When you sit on a Zorblast Whoopee Cushion you're going to experience something very different. Roar with laughter as you watch your "chum" bonds at the molecular level to the cushion and they both float into the air. He'll bounce around the ceiling like a balloon until the cushion lowers him to the ground, with a satisfying "farty" sound.

Have you heard of the old fashioned, dull exploding cigar? Try the Captain's updated version. The Zorblast Cigar samples your "crony's" DNA during the first puff. Seconds later the cigar takes off and pursues the smoker around the room burning him on the butt, for at least an hour.

Or Captain Zorblast's Pheromone capsules. Simply drop a capsule into a drink or some food and roar with laughter as you watch your "buddy" attract dogs, cats, ants, wasps, men, women (Contact the Captain for a full list) like a sexy magnet.

Maybe Zorblast's Expanding Laxative. Think of the fun! One dose of this remarkable potion will produce a room full of multicoloured foam produced from your "amigo's" fundament. He'll never be the same again!!!

There REALLY are too many fabulous things to list here, so

call the Captain! You know it makes (non) sense!!!
— Andy Brown

For Sale—Pets

For Sale: Collection of genetically altered zombies. Be mindful when asking about the price. Email: Friendly.Z.Man@Z.Com
— Andrew Browning

Adoption Opportunity: Four-headed lab accident who answers to Captain Pancake. We still consider him a dog. Great companion ... just eats other dogs (don't ask the neighbors). Performs complicated tricks! Email: Dr.It.Was.Not.Me@thx.edu
— Andrew Browning

For Sale—Remedies

Uncle Takahara's Immortality Brew. From the creators of Uncle Takahara's Timestop Watch and Uncle Takahara's Forever Youthful Tincture comes a new potion designed to keep the drinker alive for as long as it is consumed regularly. Ask your local chemist or write to Uncle Takahara/PO Box 1407/Springfield, MO 65801.
— Amanda Partridge

For Sale—Vehicles

For Sale: Study advanced technology with an unflyable extraterrestrial spaceship. Unique features include talking seats, furry interior, and liquid fuel cells (mostly runs on bodily fluids, such as blood). Good condition. Starting price—top-secret clearance required. Please contact via cryptic messages to space probes.
— Andrew Browning

Help Wanted

WANTED: Research Assistant. No advanced degree required. Familiarity with leviathan majoris preferred. Ability to fire tranquilizer gun underwater a must. If interested, email p.albescu@wmu.edu.

— Amanda Partridge

WANTED: Pest Control, one that works on rabbit/nixie crossbreeds. Husband toyed with genetic mixture, and now the vermin have infested our home. Please call (555) 555-5555 with solutions.

— Amanda Partridge

For Escape Artists Only: Unfortunately, I've entombed myself inside a standard sized test tube, measuring 18 X 150 mm. This was a shrinking experiment gone awry. Fortunately, I'm still intelligent enough to disseminate this message, even though I'm currently stranded in an unsuitable location. However, with that said, I still don't know how to actually get out of here. Assistance would be greatly appreciated. Theoretically, a minimum IQ of 125 is required in order to successfully complete this task—that's an educated guess, though. Help! Please direct replies to Box 377, Complex Clinical Laboratories, Classified.

— Andrew Browning

Grave Robbers Wanted: I'm looking to conduct what I call "soul-transferring experiments" to corpses. However, I did not receive my grant this year (or any year prior, to be specific). Still, this is a legitimate once-in-a-lifetime opportunity for an otherworldly experience! Just need some help snatching up those corpses! FYI, I'll be transferring your soul to a corpse. Email: Soul.Full@ethereal.com

— Andrew Browning

Frantic Chemical Specialist Needed: Looking for a maniacal chemist. No questions necessary. Email: Dr.Phooey@chem.edu

— Andrew Browning

Experienced Minion Required: Help wanted due to an unexpected severance—laboratory minion and dogs-body with own teeth, all parts in working order and no outstanding warrants for their arrest. This exiting vacancy is a once in a Blood Moon opportunity, for a one-year trial period, which may or may not be extended—subject to performance. Ghouls need not apply. This includes Mrs. Doris May Clackle-Bucket from Lower Knurdling-on-the-Marsh.

The successful candidate must like animals and sentient, homicidal plants, have a clean driving license, and remain calm under pressure—for example, angry villagers waving lit torches and pitchforks, Acts of Gods, demonic possession, or alien invasion.

Generous rates of pay: £850 ($1200) per annum before tax and a rent-free, partially furnished broom cupboard, to be shared with an extended family of genetically modified wolf spiders and a delusional mouse.

Must provide excellent references and survive a competitive selection process. Applicants who make it to this stage are guaranteed decent burial should they be unsuccessful at interview, with sincere condolences to any surviving family—or their creators. Please note: this expression of sympathy will not involve monetary compensation of any kind.

Professor Tiberius Earwig Ph.D., FGS

— Rebecca Siân Pyne

Personals—Romantic

Missed Connection: Walking Robot Rover Meets Yellow Galoshes. I was testing my astroprojection machine with a stroll downtown, you were walking your grey robo-labrador. We made eye contact and stopped to talk, but my voice did not project with the rest of my person. It may have been the out of body experience, but I know I felt something. If you did, too, email jalvarez@hotmail.com with the name of your dog in the subject line.

— Amanda Partridge

Services Offered

Stolen Identity? Have you been replaced by a being that walks like you, talks like you, and has your friends and family convinced it is you? We can help. Call (123) 456-7890 to get your life back.

— Amanda Partridge

Madame Salome's Escorts: It happens to us all ... That last minute party invitation ... Perhaps a wedding or a funeral ... The unveiling of a death ray or a new piece of genetic tinkering ...

And the invite says, "Plus one."

You're too busy to form long term relationships, so give Madame Salome a call. She can provide that elusive "Plus one."

Someone supernaturally elegant to impress your peers? Madame Salome's contacts among the mysterious elf cultures are sure to fit the bill. Sha'thena is six feet tall with long flowing hair that brushes against her ankles. Her eyes are dark as coals, and she is willowy and elegant. Elves are notoriously arrogant, but they are breathtakingly gorgeous. Sha'thena will not talk at all during the event but will give the impression that she finds you mildly less beneath her contempt than anyone else in the room.

Not sure what look you want? Try a succubus. Succubi take on the form of any man's fantasy and will spend the event fawning over you and hanging on your every word. Madame Salome provides a unique potion that will force the succubus to remain in your chosen form. In the event of the potion wearing off, the succubus will pick up on every male fantasy in the room and will morph into a truly disturbing variety of forms. Any client who is in any way ambiguous about his sexuality may well find it clearly displayed at an inopportune moment.

Perhaps your tastes run to the more subservient. We have a number of pale, wistful, dreamy, slightly aristocratic young ladies who will cling obsessively to your arm and gaze adoringly into your eyes, only occasionally sighing. Many clients find the constantly moist eyes and simpering behaviour very attractive, and so we ask that they sign a waiver guaranteeing that they will continue to pay Madame Salome's fee for no fewer than three months.

And, of course, Madame Salome doesn't forget our lonely ladies. Female clients should explore our range of incubi. Please read our succubus section for possible areas of incompatibility.

Madame Salome represents a number of vampire counts who are desperate for female companionship. These fellows are moody, introspective, and very sophisticated. Potential clients should ensure that any event is held during the hours of darkness and should not feature food flavoured with garlic.

Perhaps an escort with a rougher edge? A werewolf companion would definitely fit the bill. These gentlemen are dark, brooding, and overtly passionate. Expect a great deal of attention during the event. Clients should be aware that werewolves can be very possessive of their companions and will react adversely to even the most casual flirtation from any other men. The degree of the reaction is dependent on the phase of the moon, so check your ephemeris.

You don't have to be lonely with Madame Salome.

— Andy Brown

Tarquin Soopah: Bespoke Tailor to the Discerning Gentleman

The Bard wrote, "For the apparel oft proclaims the man" and indeed, it is still true. Because Tarquin Soopah makes the clothes that truly proclaim the man.

Imagine the effect of walking into a crowded room garbed in a jacket made from human skin. Mr Soopah and his team apply tattoos to the jacket to ensure total originality.

If you feel the cold, choose from Tarquin Soopah's selection of yeti skin coats. Yeti skins are remarkably varied in the wild and range from blue-black through to creamy white, including mottled patterns.

For the gentleman who likes to make an entrance, Tarquin Soopah makes a comprehensive range of trousers using giraffe, zebra, tiger, panda, gerbil, and hamster skin, to name but a few.

Mr Soopah's millinery department has sourced mammoth skins, and they offer caps, fedoras, Stetsons, and kepis. For extra waterproofing, Mr Soopah offers the same range made from mermaid scales. This also adds a highly decorative effect for the discerning customer.

Tarquin Soopah caters to every size and shape of gentleman, from skinny midget to obese troll. Contact Tarquin Soopah for an appointment and be the fellow you want to be.

— Andy Brown

Wanted—Test Subject

Wanted: An uneducated test subject who's willing to volunteer in a time traveling experiment to an undisclosed yet also historically violent event. No experience needed. Helmets will be provided. Safety not guaranteed. Contact information: We'll contact you in due time.

— Andrew Browning

ABOUT

BIOS FOR CLASSIFIEDS AUTHORS

Andy Brown is a musician and entertainer living near Edinburgh in Scotland. (He doesn't currently own a kilt but does play bagpipes a little.) He is a pleasant enough fellow with a healthy interest in many things and an obsessive interest in many others. (Music, computers, astronomy, reading, writing…) He plays a wide variety of instruments to a wide variety of standards. His greatest happiness is his family and the fact that he wakes every morning still breathing. His greatest sadness is that he might die before warp travel, teleportation, and Klingons are discovered.

~

Andrew Browning doesn't like to "wordsmith"—he prefers literary kung fu. He lives in the suburbs of Cincinnati, Ohio, where he works as a copywriter at an advertising agency. When he is not writing, he is failing at golf. You can follow him on Twitter at @AndrewRBrowning

~

Amanda Partridge is a paralegal in small town, Arkansas, where she is active in several local literary organizations. She received her B.A. in English in 2011. When she isn't writing legal documents, Amanda dabbles in short stories and poetry.

~

Dr Rebecca Siân Pyne is a writer, researcher (and mental health first-aider), now based in West Wales, via Cardiff University and the Swiss Federal Institute of Technology, Zurich. She has a a PhD in Micropalaeontology, specializing in British Upper Cretaceous ostracods, with published research in *Revista Española de Micropaleontología* and *Palaeogeography, Palaeoclimatology, Palaeoecology*. Short stories have appeared in *Bête Noire, Macabre Cadaver, Bards and Sages Quarterly, Albedo One, Aurora Wolf, Eschatology, Neo-Opsis*, and others. Research assistants include a mad sprollie (springer spaniel x collie) who ensures there is no time for writer's block.

ABOUT THE EDITORS

In addition to editing *Mad Scientist Journal,* Jeremy Zimmerman is a teller of tales who dislikes cute euphemisms for writing like "teller of tales." He is the author of the young adult superhero book, *Kensei.* Its sequel, *The Love of Danger,* is now available. He lives in Seattle with a herd of cats and his lovely wife (and fellow author) Dawn Vogel. You can learn more about him at bolthy.com.

~

Dawn Vogel has written and edited both fiction and non-fiction. Her academic background is in history, so it's not surprising that much of her fiction is set in earlier times. By day, she edits reports for historians and archaeologists. In her alleged spare time, she runs a craft business and tries to find time for writing. She lives in Seattle with her awesome husband (and fellow author), Jeremy Zimmerman, and their herd of cats. Visit her website at historythatneverwas.com.

ABOUT THE ARTIST

Luke Spooner a.k.a. 'Carrion House' currently lives and works in the South of England. Having recently graduated from the University of Portsmouth with a first class degree he is now a full time illustrator for just about any project that piques his interest. Despite regular forays into children's books and fairy tales his true love lies in anything macabre, melancholy or dark in nature and essence. He believes that the job of putting someone else's words into a visual form, to accompany and support their text, is a massive responsibility as well as being something he truly treasures. You can visit his web site at www.carrionhouse.com.

61953059R00092

Made in the USA
Lexington, KY
24 March 2017